A Book of
Magic Adventures

A
BOOK OF
MAGIC
ADVENTURES

Ruth Manning-Sanders

DRAWINGS BY
ROBIN JACQUES

METHUEN CHILDREN'S BOOKS

also by Ruth Manning-Sanders

A BOOK OF GIANTS
A BOOK OF DWARFS
A BOOK OF DRAGONS
A BOOK OF WITCHES
A BOOK OF WIZARDS
A BOOK OF MONSTERS
A BOOK OF GHOSTS AND GOBLINS
A BOOK OF DEVILS AND DEMONS
A BOOK OF CHARMS AND CHANGELINGS
A BOOK OF OGRES AND TROLLS
A BOOK OF SORCERERS AND SPELLS
A BOOK OF SPOOKS AND SPECTRES
A BOOK OF ENCHANTMENTS AND CURSES
A BOOK OF MARVELS AND MAGIC
A BOOK OF MAGIC ANIMALS
A BOOK OF CATS AND CREATURES
A BOOK OF KINGS AND QUEENS
A BOOK OF PRINCES AND PRINCESSES
A BOOK OF HEROES AND HEROINES
RUTH MANNING-SANDERS
FOLK AND FAIRY TALES
GIANNI AND THE OGRE
SCOTTISH FOLK TALES

*First published in Great Britain 1983
by Methuen Children's Books Ltd
11 New Fetter Lane, London EC4p 4EE
Copyright © 1983 Ruth Manning-Sanders
Illustrations copyright © 1983 Robin Jacques
Set in Great Britain by
Wyvern Typesetting Ltd, Bristol
Printed by Butler & Tanner Ltd,
Frome, Somerset*

ISBN 0–416 24520 X

British Cataloguing in Publication Data

Manning-Sanders, Ruth
  A book of magic adventures.
  I. Title   II. Jacques, Robin
  823'.914 [J]   PZ7

Contents

1 Wide Awake and his Brothers *Iceland*   page 7
2 The White Goat *Germany*   18
3 The Goblin Mule *Macedonia*   34
4 The Adventures of Sven *Denmark*   41
5 White Doviekin *Pomerania*   66
6 The Barrel Man *Czechoslovakia*   75
7 Silver Hoof *Russia*   89
8 The Dwarf in the Storm *Switzerland*   97
9 The Old Man and his Three Daughters *Russia*   101
10 The Gypsy and The Dragon *Transylvanian Gypsy*   109
11 The Miller and the Devil *Flanders*   118
12 The Fiddler in Hell *Russia*   122

1. Wide Awake and his Brothers

1. The Magician's Gifts

Once upon a time there lived a husband and wife who had five sons. And when the boys were just old enough to be left by themselves, the husband and wife went out into the meadows to mow, leaving the boys at home. And there came an old man knocking at the door.

'I am very thirsty,' said the old man. 'Can you spare me a drop of water?'

'We can spare you better than water,' said the eldest boy. 'We have plenty of milk, and if you are hungry, we can give you bread and meat as well. But you look tired, sir. I think you must have walked a long way. Come in, and sit down and rest a while.'

So the old man went in and sat down in an armchair in the parlour, and the boys were tumbling over each other in their eagerness to bring him food and drink, for they were kind-hearted lads. The old man ate and drank ravenously; and when he had finished his meal, he thanked the boys and asked them their names.

'We haven't got any names,' said the eldest boy.

'No names!' said the old man. 'Then what do your parents call you?'

'Oh, just first, second, third, fourth and fifth,' said the boy.

'Nay, nay, that won't do!' exclaimed the old man. 'Stand here in a line before me, and I will christen you.'

The boys thought this was great fun. They formed up in a line, like little soldiers; and the old man went from one to the other, touched each one on the shoulder and named him. To the first he said:

'You shall be called Wide Awake,
And wide awake shall you be.

Be it far, be it near,
Be it dark, be it clear,
Yet all things shall you see.'

And to the second he said:

'You shall be called Good Swordsman,
And a good swordsman shall you be.
The sword you hold shall make you bold
To strike the enemy.'

And to the third he said:

'You shall be called Tracker,
And a tracker you shall be.
No winding trail shall make you fail
To track the enemy.'

And to the fourth he said:

'You shall be called Good Climber,
And a good climber shall you be.
No cliff too steep, no gorge too deep –
You'll reach the enemy.'

And to the fifth he said:

'You shall be called Eloquent,
And eloquent shall you be.
The words you say shall have their way
In any company.'

'These names I give you with my blessing,' said the old man.
And then – well, what do you think? He disappeared. First he was
there, and then he was gone, to the utter astonishment of the boys.
'He must be a saint, or an angel,' said the eldest boy.
'Or a magician,' said the second.
'But if a magician, then I'm sure a good one,' said the third boy.
'Yes, yes, for he gave us good names,' said the fourth.

'But I'm not sure what eloquent means,' said the fifth boy.

'It means – ' began the first boy, whom the old man had named Wide Awake. But then he saw his father and mother coming back from the fields, and he ran to them and said, 'Did the fox do much damage?'

The parents were astonished; for there *had* been a fox in the fields – but how could the boy know that?

And when they asked him, he rubbed his hand across his eyes, and said, 'I think – I saw him.'

2. The Troll

Now our story takes a jump over the next few years; and when we meet the five brothers again, they have grown into five fine, sturdy young men, and have taken service in the king's stables.

But in the royal palace all is misery and confusion; for, despite everything that armed guards and night watchmen and blazing lights could do, four of the king's young daughters have been stolen away by night, one after the other. Now there is only one princess left, and her distracted parents can think of no way of protecting her. The thefts always took place on a certain night, a cold night in March, just before Easter, and you may be sure that on that night every lamp in the palace was lit, and no one went to bed, except the princesses. But at midnight – what do you think? – every light went out, and willy-nilly, everyone fell asleep, wherever they might be: the armed guards pacing the corridors dropped to the floor and slept; the maids, sitting on hard chairs in the princesses' bedroom, nodded, shut their eyes, opened them again, yawned, nodded their heads, shut their eyes again, and slept. The king and queen themselves tried to keep awake, the king reading an exciting story to the queen, whilst she sat embroidering some elegant tapestry. But just before midnight the book dropped from the king's hand, and the tapestry fell from the queen's knee – and there they were both fast, fast asleep. . . . And when everyone woke in the morning another princess had vanished. And now only one was left.

And on Easter Eve Wide Awake said to his brothers, 'What is my name worth, and why was it given to me if I also must fall asleep at some demon's bidding? Surely it is I who must keep watch this Easter Eve, and catch and fight that thief if he comes to steal our princess. Be he imp, or wicked fairy, or Old Nick himself he shall not put *me* to sleep, I promise you!'

'And I,' said the second brother, 'why is my name Good Swordsman, if not to fight and kill this wretched thief?'

'And I,' said the third brother, 'is not my name Tracker? Should the thief escape my brother's sword and flee away, shall I not be able to track his footsteps, be they ever so faint?'

'And I,' said Good Climber, 'be the thief more agile than a mountain goat, is there any cliff I cannot scale, or any precipice so steep that I cannot follow him down, should he descend it?'

'And I,' said Eloquent, the fifth brother, 'when we come up with the thief, however cunning he may be, and even if he should escape my brother's sword – am I not called Eloquent? And shall not my words prevail even though swords may fail?'

And on that day before Easter the five brothers went to the king and asked for permission to watch in the princess's room and try to catch the thief. The king willingly gave permission though he had not much hope that any good would come of it. 'My brave lads, you will only fall asleep like all the rest of us,' he said.

'Your Majesty, *I* shall not fall asleep. My name is Wide Awake,' said the eldest brother.

'Names, names!' cried the king, 'what are names that we should trust in them? But there, go and do your best.'

So, that night, the five brothers went into the princess's bedroom, where the young princess, bless her heart, lay sleeping peacefully.

'Now, brothers,' said Wide Awake, 'I am the eldest of us, and I pray you to be guided by me. You, Tracker, and you, Good Climber, and you, Eloquent, hide yourselves in yonder big cupboard. But you, Good Swordsman, stand with me here by the window with your sword in your right hand and this darkened lantern in your left hand. And when I call out "Strike!" swing up the lantern, strike with your sword and cut off the thief's head, or the arm in which he carries the princess, whichever you can most quickly reach.'

'That I will do, you may trust me, brother,' said Good Swordsman.

So in the dark they waited, for one hour, for two hours. And then, at the stroke of midnight, the window was opened by a huge hand and into the room stepped a gigantic Troll. One stride of his long legs, and he was at the princess's bed. Now he had her in his arms, now he was striding again towards the window.

'Strike!' shouted Wide Awake.

And Good Swordsman swung his lantern and struck with his sword. But he could not reach the Troll's head, because, stooping as that Troll was, his head all but touched the ceiling; nor dared he strike the Troll's right arm lest he wound the princess. So, with a leap, he struck at the Troll's left side and cut through the thick leather jacket and wounded the Troll's left arm.

With a yell that shook the palace, but still clutching the princess with his right arm, the Troll leaped out through the window and fled away into the night.

'After him, brothers, after him!' shouted Wide Awake. 'Tracker, you lead the way!'

Now Tracker, Good Climber, and Eloquent were out of the cupboard. Now, one after the other, the five brothers had scrambled out through the window; now, led by Tracker, they were racing through the night. A waning moon, shining in a cloudless sky, gave them a little light, just enough to prevent them from bumping into rocks or trees, though not enough to show them any traces of the Troll's footsteps. But Tracker never hesitated. He was as sure of the way he should go as any blood-hound. And on and on ran the brothers, guided by Tracker's voice, until they came to the bottom of a cliff, so steep, so high, that its top seemed almost to reach the moon.

'Now it is my turn!' cried Good Climber. 'I have a rope here round my waist. I will go up the cliff, and let down the rope, and pull you all up, turn by turn.'

That Good Climber did. And by and by, there they were, all five, standing at the top of the cliff.

What now? From the top of the cliff they looked down over a bleak desert land; and far off they saw lights shining from what seemed to be a huge building.

'Ah,' said Wide Awake, 'that must be the Troll's castle; and if you, Good Climber, will let us down from this cliff, I think Tracker will find the shortest way across the desert.'

So with his rope, Good Climber let his brothers down, one by one, and followed them himself, leaping from rock to rock and over great chasms in the hill face, more nimbly than any mountain goat. And then, guided by the blaze of lights, they crossed the desert, and arrived close to the Troll's castle just before daybreak.

The huge castle stood on a hill, but you may be sure that hill was soon climbed. And now here were the brothers, all five of them, standing under the castle walls.

But there was something rather strange about that castle. On the north side the windows were all ablaze with lights, and a lighted lantern hung over the huge entrance door on that same side. But there were no windows, nor were there any lights, on the other three sides of the castle.

'I wonder why this should be?' whispered Tracker.

And Wide Awake whispered, 'That is easily explained. Our enemy is a Night Troll, and if a Night Troll sees but one blink of the sun, he is immediately turned into stone.'

'Oh ho,' said Eloquent, 'then I think I see how to manage this business, and free the princesses, without your having so much as to draw your weapon from its sheath, Good Swordsman. You can leave this matter to me, my brothers. So stay where you are, and do not come until I call.'

'But it may be that you will run into great danger,' whispered Good Swordsman. 'And what is my sword for but to protect my brothers?'

'There are times, brother,' whispered Eloquent, 'when my tongue is mightier than your sword, and such a time is this.'

'I think,' said Wide Awake, 'that Eloquent must be right, and that we should do as he bids us.'

'Yes, let us do as he bids us,' whispered Tracker and Good Climber.

So it was four against one; and Good Swordsman sheathed his weapon, though very unwillingly. Then he, with Wide Awake, Tracker, and Good Climber waited in the darkness under the south side of the castle; and Eloquent walked boldly forward to where, on the north side, the windows gleamed with light, and a huge lighted lantern hung over the entrance door.

Rat-a-tat-tat! Eloquent grasped the knocker, and knocked with all his might. *Rat-a-tat-tat!* RAT-A-TAT-TAT!

The door opened. There stood the Troll, with his left side and arm swathed in bandages, and a furious scowl on his face.

'What do you want?' he roared.

'A thousand, thousand pardons, your High and Mightiness,' said Eloquent, with a long bow. 'I and my four comrades are travelling to behold the wonders of the world. We propose to write a book, which shall describe all these wonders. In it your High and Mightiness and your marvellous castle must of course be noted down. In fact, I think it will make the most interesting chapter in the whole book.'

'Um, um,' growled the Troll.

'If you would permit me to ask you a few questions –' said Eloquent.

'Um-m,' growled the Troll again. 'Well, ask on.'

'You are, I believe, the strongest being in all the world?' said Eloquent.

'So folk say,' nodded the Troll.

'And is not that a glorious thing to be?' said Eloquent.

'Um, um,' nodded the Troll.

So Eloquent went on talking and flattering until he had the foolish old monster grinning with delight, and inviting Eloquent to come in and breakfast with him. But Eloquent was keeping a watch on the sky, and when he saw a little glow of light there, he swung round to the east, and cried out, 'Oh see, your High and Mightiness, what a lovely maiden is coming up the hill! Surely she must be your daughter?'

'My daughter!' growled the Troll. 'What do you mean? I have no daughter. But if she's a beautiful maiden, she's the maiden for me!'

'Then come and look! Come and look!' cried Eloquent, hurrying to the eastern side of the castle.

And the Troll followed him.

What happened? The rising sun shone full on the Troll's face – and he turned into a pillar of stone.

'Brothers! Brothers! Brothers!' shouted Eloquent.

The four brothers heard. They came running. But the Troll's wife also heard, and she came pounding out of the door.

'Where is my husband?' she yelled.

'Just round the corner, dear madam,' said Eloquent.

The Troll's wife hurried round the corner of the castle. She saw the stone pillar. She gave one tremendous howl. But that was the last sound she ever uttered: for the rising sun shone full upon her; and she too became a pillar of stone.

3. The Five Princesses

'Three cheers for brother Eloquent!' shouted Wide Awake and Good Swordsman, and Tracker, and Good Climber.

'But,' said Wide Awake, 'we have still to find the princess.'

'Then follow me into the castle,' said Tracker.

And the five brothers trooped in through the wide open entrance door.

Through one room and through another room went Tracker, followed by his brothers. 'There are footsteps here, and footsteps there,' said Tracker, 'but these are not the footsteps of any princess. Ah, of course, our friend the Troll would have been carrying her.'

'Not surely into any of these grand rooms!' said Wide Awake. . . . 'But look, brother, isn't that a glimmer of light coming up through the floorboards?'

'You are right, brother,' said Tracker. 'And here are the Troll's footsteps going down a flight of stairs.'

So, led by Tracker, and each one holding another's hand, the brothers cautiously made their way down a steep flight of stairs. And as they went that little glimmer of light became ever bigger and brighter, until, at the bottom of the stairs they came to a door with a lantern hanging over it. The door was locked, but the five brothers flung their weight against it, and crashed it down; and stepping over it came into a narrow room where – oh the pity of it! – five princesses sat on five hard stools against the wall, each one with her golden hair gathered up into a tight knot and tied to a peg on the wall. They had one of the Troll's huge shirts spread out between them, and they were busy mending holes in it.

'No, no, no!' they cried, as the door crashed down, 'we haven't finished it, but we are doing our best, indeed we are. Oh do not, do not beat us!'

But Eloquent said gently, 'Dear princesses, the Troll will never beat you again.'

'And we are here to set you free,' said Wide Awake.

Then, oh so gently, so tenderly, Good Swordsman cut the princesses' golden hair free of the pegs. And oh how the princesses jumped for joy, and clapped their hands, and laughed, and cried out, 'We are free, we are free!' And how, too, they flung their arms about their rescuers; and yes, ignoring any royal etiquette, how they hugged and kissed them!

And so, in merry mood, they all scrambled up the stairs again, and hurried through one grand room, and through another grand room, and into the entrance hall, and out through the great front door.

But now came the problem – how to get the princesses home again? For of course the Troll, with his tremendous strides, had had no use for horses. There was no help for it: the poor, half-starved, weary little princesses must foot it, like any begger maids, over the bleak desert, and up the monstrous cliff, and among the rocks and forest trees.

'But we will give you all the help we can, dear princesses,' said Tracker. 'We will lift you over the difficult places, and when you are weary we will sit and rest.'

'Ha! ha! ha!' came a chuckling laugh. And there before them stood the old magician, who had long ago given the five lads their names.

'Bravely done, my hearties!' said he. 'But now it is my turn. Take hands, a lad and a lass, a lad and a lass, and stand round me in a circle. . . . Good, good,' he went on, as they hastened to obey him. 'Now, loudly and clearly, repeat these words after me:

'*Kindly sunbeams, we entreat*
That you lift us off our feet.'

'*Kindly sunbeams, we entreat*
That you lift us off our feet,'

they all cried in chorus.

And then what happened? They all rose up into the air.

'Good, good,' chuckled the old magician. 'Now just two more lines:

'*Kindly breeze, we bid you come*
To carry us swiftly and merrily home.'

And as, hovering over the old magician's head, the five brothers and the five princesses had repeated these lines, there they were going through the air at such a speed that in no time at all, as it seemed, they had reached their home, and were floating through an open window of the palace into a room where the king and queen sat dolefully over an untasted breakfast.

'Mother! Father! Here we are!'

What joy, what happy tears, what hugging and kissing, what half-sobbed out words of thanks and gratitude to the five brothers! And when the news of the princesses' rescue spread through the palace, what shouts and cheers echoing through all the rooms, and out in the palace gardens, and even through the streets of the king's city!

Can you guess how our story ends? Yes, of course: here are five beautiful princesses and five gallant lads – how should it end but in five happy weddings?

Among the guests, of course, were the lads' father and mother, upon whom the king bestowed such a handsome sum of money that they had no need to do another stroke of work unless they pleased.

And there was another guest, who came uninvited, because no one knew his address. Guess who that was? Yes, you're right; it was the old magician: dressed for the occasion in such a magnificence of velvet robes and glittering jewels as almost made one blink to look at him.

But when, after the ceremony, the king sought him out to thank him for saving his daughters – he couldn't be found anywhere. He had vanished, according to his usual custom. But I know, and you know, that he must still be somewhere in the world, where, if some things turn out badly, a great many things turn out well. And how could that be, without his help?

2. The White Goat

1. The Cottage in the Forest

One moonlit evening Michel, the charcoal burner, was driving home through the forest in his little cart. He was driving slowly, for the way was rough, what with the tree roots and the moss-covered stones; and Michel's big dog, Baz, was running ahead, and coming back to the cart, and running ahead again.

'Oh dear me, are we *never* to get home?' Baz was saying.

And then, after one such running ahead, Baz didn't come back. He stood sniffing at something that lay on the ground. He was wagging his tail, and gently whimpering.

'Hey, Baz, old chap, what have you found?' said Michel, urging on the pony. But when he saw what Baz had found, he pulled up the cart, and jumped down in a hurry.

Lying there on the ground was a young girl. The moon shining through the tree branches lit up the young girl's face, and the face was lovely as any angel's.

For one horrified moment, Michel thought that the girl was dead. Then he realised that she was only sleeping; and he stooped and shook her gently.

The girl gave a sigh, opened her eyes, and looked up at him.

'My dear,' said Michel, 'you mustn't sleep here. Don't you know that there are wolves in the forest?'

'If there are wolves then let them come and eat me!' said the girl. And she burst into tears. 'As good to be eaten by wolves as to die of hunger,' she sobbed.

'Nay,' said Michel, 'you shall neither be eaten by wolves, nor shall you die of hunger. You shall come home with me; and my old wife, Nicky, shall give you supper and a bed.'

'Are there then kind people still left in this weary world?' said the girl. And she let Michel lift her to her feet and help her into the cart.

Michel didn't worry her to tell her story. He drove home in silence, now and then saying to himself, 'Beautiful as an angel! Nay, more beautiful than any angel!'

And so they came to his cottage, which stood solitary in a clearing, with the forest trees standing back all round it. And there Michel helped the girl out of the cart, and brought her in to mother Nicky.

Mother Nicky didn't ask any questions; she had the girl sitting by the fire in the only armchair the little cottage possessed. And now Mother Nicky was chafing the girl's cold feet, and now she was wrapping a blanket round her, and now she was feeding her with hot soup out of a horn spoon, as if the girl were a baby. And the girl was first crying, and then she was laughing, and then she was drinking up the soup, and then she was telling Mother Nicky that her name was Roschen, and that she was an orphan, and had been trudging to town to seek for work, and had got lost in the forest, and was so tired, so tired, and – no, she couldn't remember any more.

Mother Nicky looked at Father Michel. Father Michel smiled and nodded his head.

'My dear,' said Mother Nicky to Roschen, 'you need never go a step farther. We can't give you work, for we are but poor folk. But if you will stay here with us, my old man Michel shall be as a father to you, and I will be as your mother. Often and often through the long years we have prayed to the good God to give us a child. But it seemed that the good God was not willing. And now, when we had lost hope, he has sent you. What do you say, will you stay with us?'

Then Roschen kissed Mother Nicky and said, 'Yes, I will gladly stay.'

So for three happy years Roschen lived with Father Michel and Mother Nicky, working about the little house with a will, and brightening their lives with her love and her winsome ways.

But after those three years, a strange thing happened.

It was Roschen's eighteenth birthday. Father Michel had taken a holiday, and Mother Nicky had been saving up her halfpennies for weeks to make a birthday feast. It was a beautiful sunny day; in the afternoon the three of them had picnicked by a stream in a pretty meadow beyond the forest, with big dog Baz to keep them company, and the pony cart waiting to carry Mother Nicky and Roschen home

when the sun was setting, and Father Michel walking beside the cart, smiling to himself, as he often did.

And so home, to sup on the remnants of the midday feast, with a bright fire in the kitchen, and the grandfather clock going *tick-tock* in its corner between the fireplace and the window.

And after supper, when Roschen had helped Mother Nicky to clear the table and wash the dishes, she kissed Mother Nicky and Father Michel goodnight, and went to her bed.

Roschen slept in a little room on the ground floor, leading out from the kitchen: a dear little room she thought it, because Father Michel and Mother Nicky had worked so hard to make it comfortable and pretty for her. And tonight – tired, but oh so happy! – she was quickly in bed, and almost as quickly asleep.

Tick-tock, tick-tock. In the kitchen the hands of the grandfather clock pointed to a quarter past eleven. Father Michel, who was sitting by the fire, yawned, knocked the ashes out of his pipe, and got up.

'Time we were in bed, Mother!'

Mother Nicky, who had been dozing with her feet on the fender, got up, damped down the fire, and lit a candle.

'It's been a happy day, Father Michel,' she said.

'Yes, a happy, happy day,' said Father Michel. 'And God bless the girl, say I!'

'You're right there, Father Michel,' said Mother Nicky, taking up the candle.

So off with them upstairs to bed.

All asleep now. No sound in the little house but the *tick-tock, tick-tock* of the grandfather clock in the kitchen. And then, as the clock struck twelve, Roschen sighed, stirred, and sat up in her bed, wide, wide awake.

Somebody was knocking at the window.

Roschen was a brave girl; she jumped out of bed, ran to the window, and opened it.

'Who is there?' she cried. 'And what do you want? If you are a poor traveller seeking shelter, I will call the master. But if you are a thief I will loose the dog on you!'

Yes, it was a comfort to know that big dog Baz was curled up by the kitchen fire. But it was very strange that big dog Baz should allow someone to come tapping at the window, and neither bark nor growl. . .!

And then, peering closer through the open window, Roschen saw the face of the one who had knocked. And it was the face neither of a traveller, nor of a thief, nor of man, nor of woman – it was the face of a White Goat.

The White Goat looked at Roschen; Roschen looked at the White Goat. A moment of silence, and then the White Goat speaking:

> *'Roschen, Roschen, let me in,*
> *Kiss my forehead, cheek and chin.*
> *Roschen, if you'd happy be,*
> *Give, oh give me kisses three!'*

Yes, Roschen was a brave girl, but now she was really terrified. That a *goat* should speak, that a *goat* should demand kisses of her – how should she not be terrified?

'Go away, oh go away!' she cried, and slammed down the window, ran back to her bed, and hid her head under the clothes.

There was no more sleep for Roschen that night. And in the morning she came into the kitchen looking so pale and troubled that Mother Nicky exclaimed, 'Lawks a mercy, child, what ails you?'

Roschen tried to laugh. 'I didn't sleep very well, Mother Nicky,' she said. 'I had a bad dream. I think I must have eaten too much birthday cake. But I'm all right now. . . only I had a bad dream.'

'Can't say you look all right,' said Mother Nicky. 'And what did you dream?'

'Oh, something silly about a goat,' said Roschen. And nothing more would she say. But all day long she was thinking, 'Suppose the creature should come again?' For she knew well that it was no nightmare. She knew that it was really a White Goat; and that the White Goat had spoken in the voice of a human being.

That evening, as Roschen was still looking pale and unlike herself, Mother Nicky sent her to bed early. Before she got into bed Roschen bolted her window, and drew the curtain across it. She kept her candle lighted too. But she could not sleep. She lay listening to the old folk talking quietly together in the kitchen, and to the *tick-tock* of the grandfather clock, and to its wheezy striking of the hours. When it struck ten, Mother Nicky lit a candle, Father Michel put out the lamp and they both went upstairs to bed, leaving big dog Baz sleeping before the kitchen fire.

Then Roschen tiptoed into the kitchen.

'Baz, Baz,' she whispered, 'come and sleep with me.'

Big dog Baz yawned, wagged his tail, and went with Roschen into her room. 'If it comes,' whispered Roschen, 'if that White Goat comes again, Baz, you'll drive it away, won't you?'

Big dog Baz wagged his tail again, as much as to say 'Trust me!' He lay down beside the bed and slept. Roschen got into bed, but she couldn't sleep. 'I know it will come, I know it, I know it!' she was saying to herself. . .

Tick-tock, tick-tock. The hands of the grandfather clock were moving slowly, but surely. *Tick-tock, tick-tock*: now it struck once. Half past ten. *Tick-tock, tick-tock*. Big dog Baz was quivering in his sleep, and every now and then he gave a little yelp. He was dreaming of rabbits, he was chasing those rabbits in and out among the trees in the forest. *Tick-tock, tick-tock*: the hands of the grandfather clock moved steadily on. Now it was striking eleven. Big dog Baz was still chasing rabbits in his sleep, Roschen was still wide, wide awake. *Tick-tock, tick tock*: the hands of the clock were moving on. Now the clock struck once – half past eleven! 'Don't let that creature come again,' whispered Roschen. 'Don't let it!'

Tick-tock, tick-tock. . . .

And then, as the clock struck twelve, came a knock at Roschen's window, and a voice calling out of the night:

> *'Roschen, Roschen, let me in,*
> *Kiss my forehead, cheek and chin.*
> *Roschen, Roschen, pity me,*
> *And give, oh give me kisses three!'*

Big dog Baz jumped up and ran to the window, pushing aside the curtain. Yes, there was the face of the White Goat, looking in.

'Drive it away, Baz,' whispered Roschen. 'Drive the horrid creature away!'

But big dog Baz was wagging his tail and giving happy little yelps, and through the closed window the voice of the White Goat came softly and clearly, pleading to be let in.

'I will *not* let you in! I will *not* kiss you!' cried Roschen. 'Oh you horrible creature, how dare you come here pestering me? Go away! *Go away!* Baz, Baz, why don't you drive it away?'

But Baz went on wagging his tail, and the White Goat went on begging to be let in, and Roschen went on telling it to go away. Until at last the White Goat got angry, and butted the window with his horns and broke it. And then it seemed that the whole cottage rocked. There came a sound like thunder; Roschen fell to the floor in a faint. And with a terrible cry, the White Goat turned from the window and fled away through the forest. . . .

'That was some loud thunder clap, and no mistake!' said Father Michel next morning. 'Woke me up with a start, it did. But I didn't see any lightning. Did it wake you from your sleep, Roschen?'

'N-no,' said Roschen, 'I – I wasn't sleeping, but – but my window's smashed, and – and –'

Then Roschen burst into tears, and ran to hide her head in Mother

Nicky's comfortable lap. 'Oh Mother Nicky,' she cried, 'I'm so – Oh what shall I do, what *shall* I do?'

Sobbing and shuddering Roschen told her story.

And when the story was told, Mother Nicky looked at Father Michel and said, 'Well, old man, what do *you* think about it?'

'Nay,' said Father Michel, 'my head's in a whirl. I can't think straight at all. But if you've a thought in *your* head, old woman, speak it out.'

'Well now,' said Mother Nicky, 'one thing is certain sure. The animal is no devil's goat, because white is the angel's colour, and I think the animal should have hearing. So my advice to you, Roschen my darling, is this: if the Goat comes again tonight, do as it asks you. What harm can come of kissing the poor creature? Of course it may not come again, and then that will be the end of it. But don't get into bed till after midnight strikes. Best way sit quietly by the kitchen fire. And don't undress yourself neither. For it is not fitting that anyone, whether man or beast, should see a maiden in her night shift.'

Father Michel nodded his head. 'That's the right of it. Dog Baz will be keeping you company. And though Mother Nicky and I will be in our bed, we'll not sleep, and if you need our help you've but to shout, and we'll be down on the instant.'

So then Roschen hugged Mother Nicky and Father Michel, and said she would do as they told her. She was a silly girl, she said, to have been so frightened. But all the same Roschen was not happy. All day she could think of nothing but the White Goat, and all day she was wishing that night might never come.

But come it did. And now Mother Nicky and Father Michel had gone up to bed; and there was Roschen sitting by the kitchen fire with big dog Baz curled up at her feet.

Everything quiet; except for the *tick-tock* of the grandfather clock, and its wheezy striking of the hours. *Tick-tock, tick-tock*; the clock struck eleven. *Tick-tock, tick-tock*, the clock struck the half hour. *Tick-tock, tick-tock* . . . Roschen was almost asleep, when, as the clock struck twelve, there came a loud knocking at the house door. . . . And then the voice out there in the night:

> 'Roschen, Roschen, let me in,
> Kiss my forehead, cheek and chin.
> Roschen, Roschen, pity me,
> And give, oh give me kisses three!'

Big dog Baz jumped up and ran to the door, wagging his tail. Roschen jumped up, ran to the door, and opened it. There in the moonlight stood the White Goat. Roschen stooped and kissed that White Goat on the forehead; she kissed that White Goat on the cheek; she kissed that White Goat on the chin. She gave those kisses in a desperate hurry, scarcely knowing what she did.

'There, I have done what you asked of me,' she panted. 'Will you please go away now, and leave me in peace?'

'No, I will never leave you,' said a laughing voice. The White Goat had certainly gone away; where it had been there stood a handsome prince, and the handsome prince was holding out his arms to Roschen.

'Roschen, you have freed me from a witch's spell – the witch who turned me into a white goat because I refused to marry her ugly daughter. Roschen, you shall be my bride. But come, now we must hurry. Three hundred miles separate me from my father's court, and if I am not there before midday tomorrow, I must be again a White Goat for another seven years.'

Then the Prince gave a whistle. And – hey presto! – there at the cottage door stood a splendid carriage, drawn by two moon-white horses.

'Into the carriage with you, Roschen, my darling,' said the Prince, 'for we must be up and away!'

'But – but, I cannot come until I have said goodbye to Mother Nicky and Father Michel,' said Roschen.

'No, no, there is not time!' cried the Prince. 'I will send for them later.' And he lifted Roschen into the carriage, jumped in himself, seized the reins, whipped up the horses. . . and now they were away, the horses galloping, galloping, and Roschen all bewildered, scarcely knowing whether she was awake or dreaming.

Upstairs in their bedroom Father Michel and Mother Nicky were lying awake. They heard the sound of those galloping hoofs, they hurried down, flung open the house door and peered out into the night. Big dog Baz was standing in the yard, wagging his tail. And far away in the moonlit distance, they saw the speeding carriage, and heard the *clip, clip, clip* of the horses' galloping hoofs.

'Our darling is gone from us forever,' said Father Michel.

'No, not forever,' said Mother Nicky. 'She will not forget us. She will come to us, or we shall go to her. I speak from my heart, and I speak true, Michel.'

'Pray heaven you may be right, Mother!' said Father Michel.

'Of course I am right,' said Mother Nicky. 'Don't you go fretting yourself. See how pleased big dog Baz is. If there was anything wrong he would not be wagging his tail. He would be growling and howling.'

2. Golden Apples, Pears, and Plums

On and on sped the carriage, the moon-white horses galloping, galloping, up hill, down hill, without stop or stay; on past towns and villages where all men slept; on past meadows where cattle stirred in their sleep, and lifted heavy heads to glimpse the carriage as it passed, and dropped their heads and slept again. The moon went down behind a distant hill, the stars faded, the eastern sky reddened with the approach of dawn; and on and on and on sped the galloping horses, urged by the Prince with whip and rein.

'See, the sun is rising, my darling,' said the Prince to Roschen, 'and now we are half-way home. But my heart misgives me. Dear Roschen, if you would let me, I would bind your eyes.'

'Oh no, no,' said Roschen, 'you shan't bind my eyes! What is there I could see that would frighten me, when I have you beside me?'

'I do not know,' said the Prince. 'But fear comes upon me like a black cloud.'

Now they are driving through a wood – such a wood as Roschen has never dreamed of. On every bush grow golden flowers, and on every tree hang golden apples. 'Oh, stop, stop!' cries Roschen. 'Do, do let me pick just a few of those golden apples!'

'No,' says the Prince. '*No!*'

'Please, *please!*' says Roschen. 'How can you refuse me?'

How indeed? The Prince reins up the horses. 'But hurry, my darling, hurry!'

Roschen leaps from the carriage, she runs from tree to tree. It seems the trees are anxious to give her their apples; it seems that they are bending their branches in reach of her uplifted hands. She fills her apron with the golden apples, and comes running back to the carriage.

'There,' says she, laughing, 'you see I did hurry!'

So into the carriage again: the Prince urging on the horses, the horses galloping – galloping with such speed that the carriage rocks.

Now past daisied meadows, now across moors where the sun lies bright on gorse and bracken frond, now down into a deep valley, and now into a second wood, even more marvellous than the first, for on every tree hang golden pears. The branches of the trees bend low, and swaying in a gentle breeze, fill the air with a ravishing perfume.

'Oh,' cried Roschen, 'Oh! Please stop one moment that I may pick some of those golden pears! Oh, if you love me, please, please stop!'

'You know that I love you, Roschen,' said the Prince. 'But I dare not stop.'

What has come over Roschen? She pouts, she frets. She has only asked him to stop for five minutes – what difference can five minutes make? She says the Prince is most unkind; she wishes she was at home again with Father Michel and Mother Nicky. *They* never refused her anything. . . .

'Neither can I refuse you anything,' said the Prince sadly. 'Only, my darling, I beg you to hurry.'

And he pulled up the horses.

See Roschen now running into the wood. See her picking pears and laying them down again, for it seems to her that this one has a bruise on it, and that one is over-ripe. . . . And so she goes deeper and deeper into the wood; until the Prince, grown desperate with waiting, leaps from the carriage, ties the horses to a tree, runs into the wood after Roschen, and brings her back.

But half an hour has passed; and though it is yet early, the day wears on towards noon, and there are still many miles between him and his father's palace.

So on they go again: the Prince urging the horses into a faster and faster gallop, the carriage rocking and swaying, the Prince saying no word to Roschen, Roschen feeling unhappy, and yet a little defiant, taking the golden pears out of her apron, and laying them with the golden apples in a pile at her feet.

Will the Prince taste an apple? she asks.

No, he will *not!*

Will he then just eat a pear, if she peels it for him?

No, he will *not!*

Well then, he needn't be angry with her, she pouts.

'Oh Roschen, I am not angry with you – only half-desperate! Roschen, Roschen, you would not have me changed again into a goat? Yet that is what will happen, my Roschen, if we do not reach my father's kingdom before noon.'

'I think we might reach the end of the world before noon, at the pace we are going,' pouted Roschen.

The Prince made no answer. He urged the horses on faster and faster, the carriage rocked and swayed; hedges, fields and farmsteads seemed to be flying backward on either side, so swiftly galloped the horses.

See now they came to yet a third wood; and in this wood the sunlight gleamed and dazzled on golden plums that hung upon the trees, and on golden flowers that edged the road, and a gentle breeze brought to Roschen's nostrils such sweet scent as might have come from Paradise itself.

'Oh, oh, I *must* have a few of those plums!' cried Roschen. 'And see, the horses are covered with foam. If you will let the poor creatures rest for five minutes, they will go all the faster.'

'Roschen,' said the Prince, 'is my fate nothing to you?'

'Of course it is everything to me,' said Roschen. 'But yet I think my wishes should be something to *you*. After all. . . .'

'After all, if it wasn't for me, you would still be a White Goat,' she was thinking. And though she couldn't quite bring herself to say it, the Prince knew what was in her mind. And now she was shedding tears, and he couldn't bear to see it. He pulled up the horses with a jerk; Roschen leaped out of the carriage. 'Only I beseech you to hurry!' he cried.

'Yes, yes, I will hurry,' called Roschen over her shoulder, as she ran from tree to tree.

The golden flowers glittered under her running feet, the golden plums hung low above her head. She stretched up her hand to one golden plum, she stretched up her hand to another golden plum, but always it seemed to her that the ripest and most beautiful of those plums were on the next tree, and on the next, and on the next. And now she was running deeper and deeper into the wood.

'Roschen, Roschen, come back!' called the Prince.

Roschen turned and waved to him. 'Just in one little minute,' she called: and ran on, until the crowding trees hid her from the Prince's sight.

The Prince waited. Roschen did not come back. He leaped from the carriage and ran after her into the wood. Oh where had she gone? He could see no trace of her.

'Roschen, come, Roschen, come. I dare not wait! Oh my Roschen, my beloved, the long miles still stretch between me and my father's court: the sun mounts in the sky, in an hour it will be noon! Roschen! Roschen! Roschen. . .!

'Roschen, I must drive on and leave you, but I will return for you before night falls. Yes, I will return, be sure of that, oh love of my heart!'

And with these last shouted words, the Prince ran back to the carriage, leaped in, whipped up the horses and drove away.

Mile after mile, mile after mile, the horses, white with foam, galloping, galloping, the Prince urging them on in desperation. See, there now in the distance glimmer the spires and domes of his father's city. Will he reach it before noon?

On, on, on! Why hamper oneself with the carriage? The Prince leaps out of it, unharnesses the horses; now he is up on the back of one, and with the other horse following is off at a furious pace. Now he is close to the city gates, but the hour hand on the great clock above the city gates points to twelve, and the minute hand is all but covering it. 'Open to your Prince, open, open!' The gates are flung wide by a startled sentinel; the Prince rides through, gallops along the high street to the palace. The first stroke of twelve sounds from the clock, the horses are in the palace courtyard, the Prince leaps from the back of the one he rides, rushes up the palace steps, in through the great entrance door . . . and as the last stroke of twelve booms from the great clock, he falls at his father's feet.

Now all the bells in the town ring out in chime after chime, and the streets are thronged with cheering people. 'Our Prince has come back to us! Our Prince, our Prince, our beloved Prince. . .!'

Yes, the spell is lifted from the Prince. Far away in a lonely place, beside a murky pool, a witch sits grinding her teeth and beating her fists in impotent rage. Yes, the Prince has outwitted her: but, ha! ha! he has lost his Roschen, and that at least is some solace to the Witch's evil soul.

Ha! Ha! The Prince has sent out a thousand soldiers to seek for Roschen in the golden wood, and bring her to the palace, but they shall not find her, no, they shall not find her, the Witch at least can manage that. . .!

Roschen has come back through the wood, carrying the golden plums in her apron. Oh me, the carriage has gone! She runs up the road a little way, and then she sees, sitting under the hedge, an old woman in a red cloak.

'Old lady, did you see a carriage pass this way?'

'Yes, little love, indeed I did, and going at some rattling pace, with a fine young man whipping up the horses.'

'Old lady, can you tell me the way to the King's city?'

'The longest way or the shortest way, little love?'

'Oh the very shortest way!'

'Well then, the shortest way is over the hedge and through the fields and across the moor, little love.'

'Then that is that way I will go. Good day to you, old lady.'

'Good day to you, little love.'

So away goes Roschen over the hedge and through the fields; and the old woman sitting under the hedge laughs to see the thousand soldiers come riding down the road in search of her.

The thousand soldiers scour the wood from end to end. They return to the King's city with the sad news that their search has been in vain. At the news the Prince faints. He is carried to bed, he is ill, very ill. The court physician shakes his head; the Queen, the Prince's mother, sits at his bedside and weeps; the King, the Prince's father, mourns; the people in the streets speak to one another in whispers: 'Has our Prince come back to us, only to die?'

And then, one day through the city gates comes a weary, weary little maiden, seeking a night's lodging, but with no money to pay for one. In her apron she is carrying golden plums. Perhaps someone will buy these plums? She wanders on to the market, and there she sees the King's cook, going from stall to stall, seeking out some delicacy that might tempt the appetite of the sick Prince.

Shyly Roschen offers her golden plums to the cook. Will he perhaps buy them for the price of a night's lodging? The cook takes a plum and tastes it. Yes, indeed he will buy the lot, and pay very well for them too! For anything so delicious he has never before tasted. So the cook takes the plums, and Roschen takes his money, and goes to an inn for a night's lodging.

For the Prince's evening meal the cook has prepared many a dainty dish; but the Prince will have none of them. In his fever he is moaning and muttering. 'Oh Roschen, where are you? Oh Roschen, my Roschen, how could you leave me?'

The Queen, who sits at his bedside, takes from a little page a plate full of golden plums which the cook has sent up – plums that fill the room with a delicious scent.

'If you do not fancy any of the other dishes, dear son, perhaps one of these plums will tempt you?'

And she puts a plum into the Prince's hand.

The Prince looks at the plum. He sits up, flinging aside the bedclothes. 'Where did you get these plums?' he cries.

'The cook bought them in the market,' answers the little page.

'Send for the cook, bring him here!' cries the Prince, leaping out of bed.

The cook is sent for, he comes hurrying. 'Where did you get those plums?' cries the Prince.

'I bought them from a little maiden in the market,' says the cook, 'but if they do not please you – '

'Please me!' cries the Prince, 'They do more than please me, they heal me of all my sickness, of all my woes! Send for the maiden, bring her here!'

Messengers are sent out, looking for the maiden. They find her in a humble lodging, they hurry her to the palace. She is frightened, she does not know what they wish of her. She pleads with them. 'If I have done anything wrong,' she says, 'I am innocent of all intention. Oh please, let me go, please let me go!'

But they will not let her go. They urge her up the stairs, and into a room where the Prince is pacing to and fro like a caged lion.

'Roschen, my Roschen!'

'Prince, oh my Prince!'

Now they are in each other's arms, and their joy is beyond all telling.

So our story comes to an end, with the wedding of the Prince and Roschen. A carriage is sent to fetch Mother Nicky and Father Michel. They put on their best clothes and are driven to the palace, and of course big dog Baz comes with them. Everyone is impatient for their arrival, because Roschen will not be married until they come.

'And how right you were, dear Mother Nicky,' says Roschen, 'when you said that white was the angels' colour; for surely no angel in heaven can be better, or kinder, or braver, or truer than my White Goat. . . .'

And far off, by a lonely pool, an old witch was beating her fists and moaning, because with all her evil spells she had not been able to turn good into evil, nor happiness into lasting sorrow.

3. The Goblin Mule

One evening the labourer, Kiril, said to his wife, 'Mara, my dear, we manage to get along now, but what will happen to us when we grow old, and I am not able to work any more?'

'Ah,' said Mara, 'what indeed? It doesn't bear thinking of!'

'But we must think of it, Mara,' said Kiril, 'and I have been thinking. Now I'll tell you what I'm going to do. You see this bag? Well, every Saturday night I'm going to put into the bag an eighth of what I have earned during the week. Then, when I am past work, we will open the bag, and we shall have enough to live on.'

'Yes, yes,' said Mara, 'you do that, my husband.'

So that's what Kiril did. Every Saturday night, for several years, he put an eighth of his week's wages into the bag. And when, at the end of eight years, he opened the bag, he found that he had saved up one hundred pounds.

Kiril's wife, Mara, could scarcely believe her eyes. She clapped her hands, she laughed for joy, and cried 'Oh, oh, oh! Now we needn't fear old age, or sickness, or anything!'

But then she had another thought. 'What if when you are away working, and I am away at market, a thief should break in and steal our hundred pounds?'

Yes, that would indeed be a calamity! Kiril thought and thought. Then he had an idea. 'How if I were to carry the money to the Duke, and ask him to take care of it for us?' he said.

Well, that seemed to both of them the best thing to do. So Kiril went to the Duke with his bag of money.

'If you please, my lord, I have a great favour to ask of you.'

'Ask without fear,' said the Duke, who was in a gracious mood.

And when Kiril told him about the hundred pounds, and asked the Duke if he would take care of it, the Duke said 'Certainly, certainly,'

and had the money, still in its bag, carried up into his treasury.

So then Kiril hurried home, well content; and he and Mara rejoiced in the thought that their money was safe.

'And I don't think we need save up any more,' said Kiril. 'What we earn now, we can spend, which means we can eat a little better, and dress a little better, and amuse ourselves sometimes at week-ends, by taking a trip into the country.'

So they did eat a little better, and they did dress a little better, and they did take an occasional trip into the country at week-ends. They spent all that Kiril earned, and were as happy and gay as any two birds in the spring time.

But then, alas, there came a day when Kiril fell ill of a fever. For several weeks he lay tossing in his bed, and when he got up again he was still too weak to go to work. 'I'll have to go to the Duke and ask for my money back,' he said to Mara. 'Pity too, but there – before we've spent the half of it, nay, before we've spent a quarter of it, I shall be strong enough to work again.'

So off with him to the Duke.

'If you please, my lord, I should like to have my money back. You see I have been ill, and – '

'*Money!*' says the Duke. 'What money?'

'The hundred pounds you were so good as to take care of for me.'

Well, did you ever? The Duke said that Kiril was raving, that Kiril had never brought him that hundred pounds. He called Kiril a rogue, and told him to take himself off, and quickly too, if he didn't want to be driven off with a whip.

Kiril staggered away. He couldn't believe it – and yet he had to believe it. And what, oh what, was he to do now?

He was going home, just about broken-hearted, when something small and green hopped out from behind the hedge. And that small green thing was a goblin.

'Well I never,' shrilled the goblin. 'Here's a pretty figure you're cutting, Kiril!'

'And so would you cut a pretty figure,' snapped Kiril, 'if you'd been cheated the way I've been cheated!'

And he sat down under the hedge, and told the goblin all about it.

'Ha! ha! ha!' laughed the goblin. 'Ha! ha! ha!'

'It's nothing to laugh at,' said Kiril.

'Oh isn't it!' said the goblin. 'Wouldn't you laugh if you could trick the Duke into giving you your money back? I'll pay you a call tomorrow morning.'

And off hops the goblin back over the hedge, scaring the sparrows with his screams of laughter.

When Kiril got home he found Mara eagerly expecting him. But when he told her about the Duke's reception of him – poor woman, how she wept! And not only did she weep, but she cursed the Duke and called him such names as perhaps no human being should call another. But when Kiril told her about the goblin she cheered up a little.

'They're powerful, those little creatures are,' she said. 'With one of those on our side, maybe we'll win through yet. Though I've nothing for your supper, Kiril, dear man, but some barley broth and a few mushrooms I've been out to pick.'

Well, they ate their supper and went to bed. They slept but poorly, being so troubled, and woke in the morning to a sunshiny world with

every drop of dew sparkling like a jewel on the grass outside the door of their cottage.

And there was the goblin turning somersaults among the dew drops.

'Kiril, Kiril, Kiril!' he was calling.

'Here I am,' says Kiril, going to the door and opening it.

And what did the goblin do then? He changed himself into a mule – the handsomest mule ever you saw! And the mule came up to Kiril and gave him a butt in the chest, not a hard butt – just a gentle one. And there was Kiril changed into the likeness of a gypsy lad – even Mara wouldn't have known it was Kiril if she hadn't seen it happening.

'Now,' says the mule, 'take me to the Duke and sell me. And mind you don't accept one penny less than a hundred and fifty pounds. Ha, ha, ha! I'm worth all that, aren't I, Kiril?'

'Ye-es, I suppose you are,' says Kiril, quite bewildered. 'But – '

'No buts!' says the mule. 'I'm master here, and you are to do as I say. If you don't think I look grand enough – how's this?'

So saying, the mule gave a skip to the right, and a skip to the left. Now there he was, saddled and bridled, with a gold saddle on his back, and a bridle studded with rubies.

'The saddle itself is worth a hundred pounds,' said the mule. 'The Duke's going to get a bargain. So it's oh, ho, ho, and off we go!'

Then Kiril, in the likeness of a gypsy lad, led the goblin in the likeness of a mule, along the road towards the Duke's palace. The Duke was having his breakfast at a table drawn up to the window in his dining hall. And when he saw the gypsy lad leading the mule along the road, he was astonished at the beauty of the creature, and at its gold saddle and ruby-studded bridle. He leaned out of the window and called, 'Hi, you, whoever you are, wait a minute!'

So the gypsy lad (Kiril) waited, and the Duke hurried out to him.

'Will you sell the animal?' said the Duke.

'Gladly, my lord Duke,' answered the gypsy lad.

'Well, how much do you want for him?'

'Two hundred pounds, my lord Duke.'

'Bah! That's too much!'

'Why, my lord Duke,' says the gypsy lad, 'the bridle alone is worth that much, and my mule is a young, strong, beautiful animal. I wouldn't be selling him at all, but that I'm poor and can't afford to keep him.'

Then the two of them begin to haggle. And when the Duke has persuaded the gypsy to accept a hundred and fifty pounds, the Duke thinks he has got the best of the bargain. So he hands over the money, the gypsy goes away, and the Duke calls for a groom to lead the mule into the stable.

'Give him oats, hay, water, and see that he has everything he needs,' said the Duke to the groom. 'He is a very valuable animal.'

The goblin-mule nearly burst out laughing. But he just managed to turn the laugh into a loud 'Heehaw!'

Next morning the groom got a message to say that my lord Duke wished to ride out, and that the mule must be saddled and bridled. So the groom brushed and combed the mule with the greatest care, and then he went to fetch the gold saddle and the ruby-studded bridle, which he had hung up in the harness room.

What did the mule do then? He lay down and rolled, so that when the groom came back he was all covered with dirt and bits of straw.

Now the groom had to brush and comb him all over again. But the mule wouldn't stand still: he reared, he plunged, he kicked. And the groom lost his temper, and gave the mule a cut with the whip. Oh ho, master mule wasn't going to stand that! He slipped off his halter, and butted his head against a crack on the stable wall. Now something very strange was happening: the mule's head and body became thinner and thinner, until they were no thicker than a piece of paper. And then that thin-as-paper mule slipped through the crack in the wall, and left only his tail hanging out.

'Help! Help!' shouted the groom in a panic, catching hold of the tail.

My lord Duke, dressed for riding, was waiting by the mounting-block in the palace courtyard. When he heard the groom shouting, he came hurrying into the stable. 'What's the matter now?' he said.

'Oh, oh, my lord,' stammered the groom, 'that – that mule – he's gone into the wall. Oh my lord, for mercy's sake catch hold of the tail, and help me to pull him out!'

'Nonsense!' cried the Duke. 'How could a mule go into that crack?'

'As I live, my lord, he did! He – he's surely the devil himself!'

The Duke stamped, the Duke swore, he caught hold of the tail, and both he and the groom began to pull.

So then what happened? The tail came off in their hands.

'I'll catch that creature if it's the last thing I do in my life!' cried the Duke. And he ordered the stable wall to be pulled down.

Well, workmen came, and they pulled down the wall. But they didn't find the mule. What they did find was the goblin. And the goblin laughed and chanted:

'The cheater cheated,
The biter bit,
The wrong made right
By a goblin's wit!'

And then the goblin turned himself into a magpie, and flew away.

The Duke sent riders scouring the country for the gypsy. But of course the gypsy wasn't found, because there was no such person. The gypsy had turned back into Kiril, and Kiril had gone home with the hundred and fifty pounds.

'The Duke robbed me of a hundred pounds, and paid me back a hundred and fifty,' he said to Mara. 'I don't exactly see the moral of it –'

'Oh bother the moral!' said Mara. 'All that matters is that we should be happy and comfortable.'

And so they were; for, strange to say, however much they spent, the hundred and fifty pounds never grew less.

4. The Adventures of Sven

1. The Mannikin on the Heath

Once upon a time there lived in Jutland a peasant, his wife and their baby son, Sven. They were so poor, so poor that the day came when they hadn't even enough to eat.

'Wife,' said the peasant, 'let us set out along the road, each in a different direction. If I can find work, well and good; if not, I must put my pride in my pocket and beg for bread. Meantime do you take our little son in your arms, and beseech all you may meet to spare us a few coins or a morsel of food. Surely somebody's heart will be moved to pity at the sight of you!'

So they set out. And at the cross roads each took a different way: the peasant going to the east; the wife with baby Sven on her back, going to the west.

The peasant's road soon brought him into a forest; and in the forest was the house of a Troll. The peasant knocked at the door of the house, and out came the Troll.

'Well, and what are you seeking?' said the Troll.

'I am seeking work,' said the peasant. 'Or if you have not work for me, at least a morsel of food for myself and my wife and our little son.'

'Oh, so you have a little son?' said the Troll.

'Yes, your honour.'

'And how old is your son?'

'Oh my lord, he is but an infant.'

'Very well,' said the Troll. 'If you will promise to give me your son when he is fourteen years old, I will give you now in exchange a never-empty purse.'

The peasant hesitated; but only for a moment. In fourteen years, he thought, anything might happen. But if he did not get help now, it was likely that even before the year was out, he and his wife and the baby would be all dead of starvation.

So he said, 'I can do no other than agree to your terms, my lord.'

'Ah,' said the Troll, 'but can I trust you?'

The peasant drew himself up. He was offended. 'I am a man of my word,' he said.

'Yes,' said the Troll, 'I believe you are. Very well – I will not ask you to sign anything. But remember, if it so happens that I do not get your son, I will take you in his place. Is that agreed?'

'It is agreed,' said the peasant.

Then the Troll handed the peasant a small green velvet purse. 'In this purse,' he said, 'there are twenty gold pieces. Not very much to be sure. But the purse has this quality, that however often you take those twenty gold pieces out of it, you will always find that it contains twenty more. And so, you see, you are now what we might call a millionaire.'

Greatly rejoicing, the peasant thanked the Troll and went home.

Meanwhile his wife, Truden, with the baby Sven on her back, in going westward had come to a heath. And in crossing the heath she met a very small mannikin, not more than nine inches high. The mannikin was sobbing, and tears like tiny dewdrops were trickling down his little brown cheeks.

The tender-hearted Truden stopped, and stooped and asked the mannikin what ailed him.

'Oh ma'am,' whimpered the tiny mannikin in his tiny shrill voice, 'all my people have left this neighbourhood. But I had perforce to stay behind, because my darling wife was about to give birth to our first baby. Now the baby is born, but my poor little wife is very ill, and there is none to tend her but myself. . . I nurse her by day, I nurse her by night; but sometimes I fall asleep from utter weariness, and then I wake in a panic to think she may be dead. And oh – oh, if I cannot get help she will die – oh she will die, she who is my life, my light, my all! Oh what can I do? What *can* I do?'

Truden felt very sorry for the mannikin. 'I don't know that I am overwise, or over-skilful,' she said. 'But if you will take me to your wife, I will give you all the help I can.'

The mannikin cheered up then. He led Truden across the heath to a mound, covered with green grass. He knocked on the mound, a door opened, and they went in to a pretty room, where a tiny little lady lay in a tiny little bed, with a tiny little baby in a tiny cradle beside the bed. It reminded Truden of a doll's house which her father had made for her when she was a little girl. And she remembered how she had once pretended that one of her dolls was ill, and how carefully, how carefully she had pretended to nurse it. Well, here was the pretence come true!

She set down her own baby on the floor, took a ball from her pocket for him to play with, and bustled into the manniken's kitchen, bade him stoke up the fire in the stove there, and finding some cold broth on the kitchen table, soon had the broth heated in a tiny saucepan. And by and by she was back beside the tiny lady's bed, with the tiny lady's head resting against her arm. And she was feeding the tiny lady with the broth out of a tiny spoon.

'Now you must sleep, my dear,' said she to the tiny lady. And laying her down, she sang, very, very softly the same old lullaby that she had once sung to her favourite doll. It went like this:

'Sleep, lovely, sleep,
Oh do not, do not weep:
The little lamb has eyes so bright,
And never, never, cries at night.
Sleep, lovely, sleep.'

The tiny lady looked up at her and smiled. Then she shut her eyes and fell asleep.

'So now,' said Truden to the mannikin, 'we can see to both the babies, yours and mine. My word, they could do with a wash!'

And she carried the babies into the kitchen, and washed her own baby in the biggest bowl she could find, and the mannikin's baby in the smallest. And then she fed them both at her breast, and laid them down to sleep, her own baby on a rug before the kitchen fire, and the mannikin's baby on her lap.

Well, with Truden's careful nursing, it wasn't many days before the mannikin's little wife grew well again, and she was out of bed and skipping about as merrily as a chirruping grasshopper. And the mannikin was shedding tears of joy and calling down blessings on Truden's head.

'Now I and my dear wife and our baby can set out to join our comrades across the sea,' he said. 'Oh yes, they will send a boat, to fetch us from the shore beyond the heath. But before we go, I have something to give you, most gracious madam.'

43

Then he went to a cupboard and took out a little packet which he handed to Truden. 'Inside this packet,' he said, 'you will find a bear's hair, a fish scale, and a bird's feather. If ever you should come to be in dire need, and know not which way to turn for help, press one of these things, the hair, the scale, or the feather, between the palms of your hands, and the King of the beasts, or the King of the fish, or the King of the birds will come to your aid.'

Truden took these three things and thanked the mannikin. And the mannikin said, 'Now hush, hush, don't say a word; I must take a look into the future.'

Truden stood very still. The mannikin shut his eyes. For a moment there was silence. Then the mannikin clapped his hands and cried out, 'I see, I see! When your little Sven grows up he will marry the king's daughter. If sorrow should come to you, dear madam, as come it may, remember what I have prophesied, and keep a brave heart. Now roll up your little son's sleeve that I may put my mark on his shoulder. For the paths of life run crookedly, and it may be that those paths will part you

44

and your son, for a time. And so, when those paths bring you together again, you shall have a mark by which you may know him.'

'As if I should ever *not* know him!' thought Truden. But not wishing to hurt the mannikin's feelings, she rolled up baby Sven's sleeve. Then the mannikin pressed his hand on baby Sven's shoulder, and when he lifted his hand again, there on the shoulder was a tiny gold-coloured star.

'As the baby grows, so will the star grow,' said the mannikin. 'And though it will never be a big mark, it will always be plain to see. And now goodbye.'

Then the mannikin's wife took her baby in one arm, and hand in hand with the mannikin walked away over the heath. So small they looked and yet so brisk, that they reminded Truden of two little birds. She watched them until they were out of sight, and then she picked up her own little son, Sven, and went home.

But when she reached home – what did she see? No poor tumbledown cottage, such as she had expected to find, but a splendid great house, surrounded by gardens bright with flowers, and orchards with trees bearing every imaginable kind of fruit. And at the garden gate stood her husband, dressed up like any prince.

'Am I dreaming?' cried Truden.

'No, not dreaming,' laughed her husband. 'Just a stroke of luck, my darling.' And he took her hand and led her into the grand house.

'But – but is this *ours*?' stammered Truden.

'Yes, it is really and truly ours,' said her husband. And he told her about his meeting with the Troll, and about the never-empty purse. But he didn't tell her about the agreement he had made with the Troll.

Truden on her part told her husband all about the mannikin, and showed him the mannikin's three gifts, and told how the mannikin had prophesied that their little son, Sven, would grow up to marry the king's daughter. And since they were not whispering, but talking loudly and cheerfully, one of the many servants who now waited on them overheard what they said. And this servant told the other servants, and the other servants told their friends; and so the news was spread far and wide – and in time came to the king's ears.

The king had a baby daughter, and he was already making plans for her future, and for the grand marriage he would by and by arrange between this little daughter and some foreign prince. So when he heard of the mannikin's prophecy, he was sorely troubled. *What*, his beautiful little princess Marikyn wed a peasant's son! No, no, that must not be: for let the peasant Olaf be now never so rich, he was still but an ignorant peasant.

'I must put a stop to this nonsense,' said the king to himself.

And he got on his horse and rode over to call upon Olaf and Truden.

They received him joyfully. And as for the king, he was all smiles and make-believe friendliness. 'What is this I hear about your little son?' he said.

So they told him, and the king said, 'Well now, if little Sven is to be my heir, we must see to his education. You must let me take him to the palace, that he may be brought up in all princely ways. You will understand that it is very important that he should have such education as befits a future king.'

Yes, they understood that. Sven's father, Olaf, was very ready to let the baby go. But Truden took a lot of persuading. 'I think a baby is best with its mother,' she said.

'Rubbish!' said the king. And 'Rubbish!' said Olaf. And they battered poor Truden with arguments. Was she so selfish as to stand in her little son's light? And so on, and so on. Until at last with a heavy sigh she agreed that the king should take her baby back to the palace with him. And shedding many tears, she put baby Sven, who was sound asleep, into his cradle. And the king lifted the cradle on to his horse, mounted himself, and rode away.

'I hope we have done right!' said Truden.

'*Right?* Of course we have done right,' said Olaf. 'What better could have happened? In time our Sven will be a king, and you and I – ah, what power we shall have in the land. . .! And as to that tiresome agreement I made with the Troll,' he said to himself, 'well – what a relief! It is all taken out of my hands. I can do nothing about it now.'

And what was the king doing? Certainly he was not making his way back to the palace. He was making his way to the banks of a swift-flowing river. And when he reached the river, he pulled up his horse, lifted the cradle – and flung it, baby and all, into the water.

'That's the end of you, you little pest!' he said.

And he rode back to the palace, well pleased with himself.

In the cradle baby Sven was still sleeping soundly. The river carried the cradle away and away, until it came to a mill. And there, just as if it knew what it was doing, the river washed the cradle up against the bank, and went on its way with many a chuckle.

By and by the miller came out of the mill. He saw the cradle, and hurried to it. Well – did you ever? – a beautiful little baby boy, fast asleep! The miller lifted the baby out of the cradle and took it in to his wife.

'Wife, wife,' he said. 'How often have we lamented that we have no child! And now see what the good God has sent us – a little son, beautiful as an angel!'

So Sven was brought up by the miller and his wife, knowing no other than that he was their child. He was still called Sven, because the miller's wife had found the name embroidered on his little shirt.

2. The Miller

The years passed peacefully over Sven's head. He grows from a pretty baby into a merry little boy, and from a merry little boy into a brave and handsome lad, knowing no other but that the miller is his father and the miller's wife his mother. In time they put him to school with the village children, where he learnt to read and write. And in time he reached his fourteenth birthday and left school to help the miller at his work.

And was he happy? No, not quite. There was a thought that troubled him – though what that thought was, he couldn't rightly say.

Meanwhile, at the palace, the baby princess, Marikyn, was growing up into a beautiful young girl. And by the time she had reached her fourteenth birthday, the king was already making plans for her marriage. There was the young king of England, there was the young Tsar of Russia, there was an Italian prince, there was the heir to the Spanish throne. Well, well, time enough in a year or two to make her choice – yes, she should make her own choice. . .!

But one day, a dreadful thing happened. The princess was walking with her maidens in the garden, when a black cloud blotted out the sun, and all was darkness. And when the black cloud lifted, and the garden became bright again – the princess had disappeared.

The king was frantic; he offered a huge reward for anyone who could find his beloved daughter and bring her home to him. And many and many a gallant knight set out in quest of her, but no one found her. The king's hair turned white. He was half mad with grief; he felt that it was a punishment for his treachery towards Sven's parents – as perhaps it was.

'Father,' said Sven one day to the miller, 'I had a strange dream last night. I dreamed that I set out to find the princess, and that after many adventures I did indeed find her – in some sort of cellar, it was. And oh Father, she was weeping, and so unhappy! I can't get the dream out of my head. I feel I must seek for her. Will you now give me your fatherly blessing, and let me go?'

'Yes,' said the miller, 'I will let you go, for I think it must be that heaven calls you. And I will give you my blessing for what it is worth. But it will not be a father's blessing. The time has come when I must tell you your history.'

And then and there the miller told Sven all about how he had found him as a baby washed up by the river in his cradle.

And Sven said, 'You are still my father; for it seems that when all the world had deserted me, you rescued me and gave me a home. And so now I will kneel at your feet to receive your blessing. And even if I should ever find my parents, they couldn't be more to me than you and your dear wife have been.'

He knelt, and the miller blessed him. And the miller's wife came out and blessed him also, calling upon heaven to guide and protect him. Then the miller gave him a little purse full of money, all he could spare, and Sven set out, walking up along the river bank. And the miller and his wife watched him until he was out of sight – he turning to wave to them from time to time.

'Our pride and joy has gone from us,' said the miller's wife, when Sven was no longer visible to them.

'Yes,' said the miller. 'But I have a feeling, dear wife, that our pride and joy will return to us, in God's good time.'

'Pray God he may!' said the miller's wife. And they went back into the mill house, a sad and lonely couple.

3. Sven finds his Mother and sets out to seek his Father

It was a bright sunny morning, and as Sven went along up the river bank that was overhung with trees, a little bird kept flying from tree to tree in front of him, and calling out 'This way! This way!' And that was very comforting to Sven; for apart from the bird's guidance, he had no notion which way to go. So, when the little bird flew out from among the trees and away from the river, and hovered over a desolate heath, still calling out 'This way! This way!', Sven left the river bank and followed the bird on to the heath.

And on the heath, beside a grassy mound, he saw a lady who sat and wept.

Sven hurried to her. 'Dear lady, why do you weep?' he said. 'Tell me, and I will help you if I can.'

'No one, no one can help me,' sobbed the lady. 'I had a husband and a Troll stole him from me. I had a son, and the king stole him from me. I am alone in the world. I had a little friend who once lived in this mound, and I came up here, thinking perhaps he might return and help me. But I have called and called, and no one answers.' She looked up into Sven's face and gave a great cry. 'Who are you, that you look at me with my son's eyes?'

'Indeed, I scarcely know who I am,' said Sven. And he told her his story. Then the lady rose to her feet and caught him by the arm.

'Roll up your left sleeve,' she said, 'and let me see your shoulder. . . Oh yes, it is there, it is there!' she cried, as Sven rolled up his sleeve. 'The little gold star that the mannikin printed upon you. You are Sven!'

'Yes, indeed, that is my name,' said Sven, all bewildered.

'But don't you understand?' cried the lady. 'You are my *son* – my dear son, Sven! Oh, I thought the cruel king had killed you! But now this makes up for all! Come, we will go home!'

And she took Sven by the hand, and brought him to the grand house that the Troll's money had built for her and her husband.

That evening she told Sven all about the Troll, and how in exchange for a never-empty purse, her husband had promised to give him Sven, when Sven was fourteen years old. And how, when after the fourteen years, the Troll had come to fetch Sven, and had not found him, he had in a rage snatched up Sven's father and carried him away in Sven's stead.

'I have still the never-empty purse,' she said. 'I am still rich; and now all the riches I possess are yours, dear son.'

So, for a week or two, Sven lived with his mother. He was happy in a way, but not entirely happy, because he was troubled about the fate of his father. And as the days passed, this trouble grew heavier and heavier, until at last he could bear it no longer. And one morning he said, 'Dear Mother, I cannot rest. How do I know but that at this moment my father may be suffering untold misery at the hands of the Troll? Or how do I know, indeed, that the Troll may not have killed him? I feel I must leave you, and find out what has become of my father. If he is alive I must rescue him; if he is dead I must avenge his death.'

His mother burst into tears and begged him not to leave her. But go Sven would, and go Sven did. Before he left, his mother put into his hand the never-empty purse; and also the bear's hair, the fish scale and the bird's feather which the mannikin had given her.

'I do not know what help the King of the beasts, or the King of the birds, or the King of the fishes may be to you,' she said. 'But the mannikin told me that you had but to rub the hair, the scale or the feather between your palms, and the creature to whom it belonged would come to your aid. And so goodbye, my dear, dear son, whom I lost and found, and now must lose again.'

'No, no, not *lose*, darling mother,' said Sven. 'Only part with for a little while.'

And having kissed his mother many times, and knelt for her blessing, which she, weeping, gave him, Sven set out.

He took the road that his father had taken all those years ago, when he first met the Troll, and came by and by into the forest. And there he overtook an old woman who was staggering along under a heavy load of wood.

'Old lady,' said Sven, 'that load of wood is too heavy for you. Come, let me carry it.'

And he took the bundle of wood from her, and walked along by her side.

'Oh,' cried the old woman, 'no one before has done me so much honour! And where might you be going, young sir, if it is not an impertinence to ask?'

'I am going to seek my father,' said Sven.

And he told her about the Troll.

'Just think of that!' said the old woman. 'I myself am servant to a Troll. And though he can't be the Troll you seek, because he has no man about the house, and no servant but myself, yet all Trolls are brothers, and know about each other's affairs. If you will come with me to my Troll's house, I will find some means of questioning him. But, oh deary me, I scarcely know how to get you into the house, because all day long the Troll, my master, sits over the front door in the shape of an owl on the watch for thieves who might come to steal the treasure he keeps in his cellar. . . . Let me think, let me think! Ah, I have it! You must wait until evening, when I go fetch the cows home. I will tie you under the

belly of the largest cow; and when I have driven the cows into the byre, I will untie you, and you can slip into the house by the back door and hide under the Troll's bed.'

So that's what Sven did. The old woman brought him within sight of the Troll's big house, and then he waited hidden among the forest trees until the evening. Then came the old woman, driving the cows from their pasture. She tied Sven under the belly of the largest cow, and drove the cows past the house round to their byre at the back. And the Troll, sitting in the shape of an owl over the front door, watched the herd go by, and counted the cows to see that none was missing.

'Why have you got a rope tied round that animal?' he squawked, as the cow, under which Sven was hidden, passed him.

'Because, my lord, the poor thing has a pain in her belly,' said the old woman. 'So I have put a rug there to comfort her.'

'Hoo!' squawked the owl. 'She is a fool, and you are another!'

But the cow, with Sven hidden under her, got safely past, and into the byre. Then the old woman loosed Sven, brought him into the house by the back door, bade him creep under the Troll's bed, and brought him some food, which he ate gratefully, for he was very hungry.

By and by the Troll came in. He was no longer in the shape of an owl. He was a huge, hideous monster.

'*Sniff, sniff, sniff!*' went the monster's nose. 'As I live,' he shouted, 'I smell human blood!'

'Ah,' said the old woman, 'there came a vulture flying over the house, and he dropped a man's bone down the chimney. I threw the bone away, but it has left its scent behind. Come, my lord, I have a tasty supper waiting for you. Eat now, for it is near your bedtime.'

Then she brought meat and bread and wine, and the Troll ate, grumbling at her all the time. 'A man's bone,' he snarled. 'A man's bone! I would I had the man here for my supper, instead of all this trash you have served up to me!'

Still grumbling he got into bed. And the old woman sat by him and told him stories until he fell asleep. . . . And then suddenly she gave such a screech that he woke up again.

'What in the Devil's name are you screeching about?' he said.

'Oh, my lord,' whimpered the old woman, 'I must have dozed off and I had such a curious dream. I dreamed of a big house in which there lived a man who had promised his son to some Troll or other. But when the Troll came to fetch the boy, the boy had disappeared, and the Troll took away the man instead. It was dreaming that I saw the poor man dragged away against his will that made me scream.'

The Troll yawned. 'You have no business to dream such things,' he said. 'But that dream happens to be a true one. It was my brother who took away the man. My word, he was in a rage at not getting the boy!'

'And where does your brother live?' asked the old woman.

'Well, he used to live near me, here in the forest,' said the Troll. 'But he has become so grand of late years that he has taken himself off and built himself a palace on an island in the sea. He is such a fine fellow that he looks upon me as a poor relation. In the daytime he takes the shape of a dragon with three crowned heads. And he has twelve sons who take the shape of crows. But every night they become Trolls again. . . . Now, enough of your nonsense! If you wake me again with your screams it will be the worse for you! I would eat you this minute, if you weren't so tough!'

Then the Troll gave a yawn that set everything in the room rattling, as if a storm wind blew through it. And then he shut his eyes and fell asleep again.

Next morning he changed himself into an owl and went to perch over the house door. Then Sven crept out from under the bed, and went with the old woman back into the byre. She tied him once more under the belly of the largest cow, and drove the cows round to the front of the house on their way to pasture. The owl counted the cows as they passed.

'If that cow doesn't get rid of the pain in her belly before tonight,' he squawked, 'I will eat her for supper.'

'Oh, I shouldn't do that, my lord,' said the old woman. 'She might not agree with you.'

'Fool!' squawked the owl. 'Foo-oo-ool!'

The old woman drove the cows into a meadow beyond the forest. Then she untied Sven.

'Be off now quickly,' she said. 'And oh, if I could but come with you! But I am kept here by a spell there is no undoing. Goodbye, dear lad, and my blessing go with you!'

4. Dragon Island

Sven walked away. He went until he came to a blacksmith's shop. And there he got the blacksmith to make him a sword. 'The very best, the very strongest, the very sharpest sword you can contrive,' he said. 'For I go to fight and kill a dragon.'

'I will do my best,' said the blacksmith. 'But I doubt if any sword will avail for that.'

However, he set to work and made the sword, and Sven was well pleased with it. He paid the blacksmith with money from the never-empty purse, and went on his way. Now he was wondering how he could get on to the island where the Troll lived who had carried away his father. Then he remembered the bird's feather which his mother had given him. He took the feather from his pocket and pressed it between the palms of his hands. In a moment, with a flurry of wings, there was King Eagle, flying down from the clouds and alighting at Sven's feet.

'At your command, young sir,' said King Eagle.

'Take me to the Dragon's island, if you please,' said Sven, scrambling on to King Eagle's back.

King Eagle spread his wings; he rose into the air; he flew, flew, over the land, over the sea, until he came to a small island. But on the island the Troll was strolling about in the shape of a three-headed dragon. And when the dragon saw King Eagle, he opened his three mouths and spat out three long streams of fire. And King Eagle had to turn and fly back to the mainland.

'I don't know how I can help you, young sir,' said King Eagle sadly.

'Never mind,' said Sven, scrambling off King Eagle's back. 'I will see what the fishes can do.'

And he took the fish scale from his pocket, and pressed it between the palms of his hands.

Immediately the sea rose in a huge white wave, and out of the wave came a Merman.

'At your command,' said the Merman.

'Please take me to the Dragon's island,' said Sven.

Then the Merman bound up Sven's mouth and nose and eyes and ears with seaweed, took Sven in his arms, and plunged with him under the waves. He swam, swam, and brought Sven to the island. And there he set him down on a pebbly beach, and unbound his mouth and his eyes and ears and nose. 'But you'll have to mind your steps, my lad,' he said. 'Even now the Troll in his dragon shape is walking about the island, keeping a look-out for intruders. You'd better hide yourself until the evening.'

Then the Merman swam away, scarcely waiting for Sven to thank him, and Sven went cautiously up the beach, and came to a meadow where the grass grew high. But he had only just reached the meadow and crouched down amongst the grass when he saw the Troll, in the shape of a huge Dragon, coming towards him. The Dragon had three heads, and on each head he wore a golden crown that glittered in the sunlight. Truly an awesome sight! But as the Dragon drew nearer and nearer, an immense flock of little birds came flying to alight on the meadow grass all round Sven, completely hiding him. And the Dragon, with an angry spit at the birds, passed by.

'And that appalling monster is the thing I have come all this way to fight!' thought Sven. 'And now I have let him pass by me!'

But he felt tired – so tired – and what were the little birds saying?

> *'Fight tomorrow, not today,*
> *Hark to what the black crows say.'*

Crows? What crows? Sven couldn't see any crows – only these little birds. But perhaps he should take the little birds' advice, and wait until tomorrow to fight the Dragon. After a night's rest he would feel stronger. He got cautiously to his feet, and looked about him for a better hiding place. And seeing an elder bush with low-growing branches not far off, he hurried to it, and hid himself beneath it.

Now the sun set, now it was evening, now it was night – a dark night and a clouded sky, showing neither moon nor stars. Sven was almost asleep when he heard a flurry of wings, and twelve crows came to perch on the elder bush above his head.

The crows were talking loudly.

'Eh, but I'm hungry!' said the first crow.

'No matter,' said the second crow. 'There'll be food enough tomorrow when father has killed Sven.'

'That he will easily do,' said the third crow. 'Maybe the miserable little fellow will try to fight, but – '

'Ha, ha!' laughed the fourth crow. 'You may well say "but"! And the miserable little fellow has had a new sword made – all to no purpose! He doesn't know – not he – that Father can only be overcome by the Man of the Mount's sword. And that sword hangs in an alcove at the back of a hall, and round the hall on seven mats lie seven huge dogs that never sleep.'

'Well, I think it's time *we* had some sleep,' said the fifth crow. 'And bed is a pleasanter couch than an elder bush. I'm off home!'

Then he flew down from the elder bush, and changed himself from a crow into a troll. The other crows did the like, and the twelve trolls went back into the palace.

'The Man of the Mount's sword,' said Sven to himself. 'How am I to get that. . .? The Man of the Mount's sword, the Man of the Mount's sword'. . . . He kept repeating the words over and over to himself in a dazed kind of way, until he fell into a troubled sleep.

5. King Bear and the Magic Sword

The light of the rising sun, flickering on his eyelids through the leaves of the elder bush, woke Sven next morning. He peered out through the branches. Everything was very quiet; no sign of life anywhere. He crept out from under the bush, and hurried to the shore. He took the fish scale from his pocket and pressed it between the palms of his hands. Then the sea rose in a huge white wave. And in the wave came the Merman.

'At your command,' said the Merman.

'I would be taken back to the mainland, if you please,' said Sven.

So the Merman, having bound up Sven's eyes and nose and mouth again, plunged with him under the water. He swam, swam, and brought Sven to the mainland.

'When you need me again,' said the Merman, 'you have only to summon me, I am always at your service. But at the moment I can be of no more help to you. You had best go into the forest, and consult King Bear.'

So Sven went into the forest, took the bear's hair from his pocket and pressed it between his two palms. Immediately – there was King Bear, ambling out from among the trees, and coming to stand before him.

'At your command,' said King Bear.

'I seek the Man of the Mount's sword,' said Sven. 'If your majesty can direct me to the place where I may find it.'

'The Man of the Mount's sword,' said King Bear. 'Nay, I have never heard of the Man of the Mount, or of his sword. But I will summon my people. Haply one of them may be able to help you.'

Then King Bear gave a roar that set all the branches of the trees rocking. And out from among the trees a host of animals came hurrying

– big animals and little animals, from the largest of lions to the tiniest of mice. They formed a circle round King Bear and Sven, and awaited King Bear's orders. But when King Bear asked them where the Man of the Mount could be found, not one of them could tell him.

'Are we all here?' asked King Bear.

'No,' piped a little hare, 'my father is missing. But – oh see, here he comes!'

Father Hare was hurrying. He had run so fast that he was out of breath. King Bear looked at him severely. 'When I call I expect *immediate* obedience,' he said. 'Why are you so late in coming?'

Father Hare tried to look penitent; but he really couldn't manage it. 'I have come a long way,' he said, 'all the way from the Man of the Mount's castle. I was skipping about there, having no end of fun, when an old woman came out of the castle. She had a glove, and when she put it on she became invisible. And she kept putting it on, and taking it off again, and appearing and disappearing. Laugh? I couldn't stop laughing, and – ha! ha! ha! the very thought of her makes me laugh now!'

'You are a flippant fellow,' said King Bear disapprovingly. 'But – well there, it's your nature I suppose, and you know no better. Now be off with you back to the Man of the Mount's castle, and take Mouse with you. Between you, you must get hold of that glove, and bring it here to Sven.'

Father Hare skipped off, and Mouse ran after him, hurrying with all her little might to keep up with Hare's swift going. King Bear dismissed the rest of the animals, and waited with Sven for Father Hare's return. 'My subjects are sometimes a great worry to me,' he said. 'But on the whole I pride myself that I can keep them in order. . . Ah, here come Father Hare and Mouse again.'

'We've got it,' cried Father Hare. 'We've got the glove! Give it here, Mouse.'

Mouse was carrying the glove very carefully, trying not to trip over it, she being so small. Father Hare snatched it from her, and pulled it over one of his paws. Immediately he disappeared. Now it was only his voice that they heard singing:

> '*Oh where and oh where has Daddy Hare gone,*
> *Oh where and oh where is he?*
> *With his tail so short and his ears so long,*
> *Oh where, and oh where can he be?*'

'Who-oop!' he cried, taking the glove from his paw and appearing again. 'Catch, Master Sven!' He tossed the glove to Sven and said, 'If you please, King Bear, I should like to go home; for my dear little wifey is cooking noodles for dinner.'

'Be off then,' said King Bear. 'We have had quite enough of your company.'

Father Hare skipped away, and King Bear said, 'Now master Sven, if you will get on my back, I will carry you to the Man of the Mount's castle. And my good little Mouse shall guide us there.'

Sven put the glove in his pocket, and they set off, Sven riding on King Bear's back, and Mouse running ahead to show them the way. They came out of the forest onto a wide plain, desolate and stony. In the middle of the plain stood a great dreary-looking castle, with grey stone walls and small barred windows, and a grim, closely-locked entrance door.

'Not an inviting sort of dwelling!' said King Bear. 'You will have to wait until night, Sven, when the watchmen come out. As they open the doors to come out, you can slip in. If you wear the glove they won't see you. And once you are inside – may heaven guide you! Keep a brave heart, and all will be well.'

Then King Bear and Mouse went back to the forest. And Sven took the glove out of his pocket and put it on his left hand. It almost scared him now to look down at himself and see nothing. 'A living, breathing Nothing – that's what I am now,' he said to himself. 'And if I couldn't see everything clearly around me, I should think I had gone blind!'

Impatiently he walked up and down, watching the sun as it travelled westward, and longing for it to set. He peered through one of the barred windows of the castle, and saw a company of Trolls sitting at supper in a huge bare hall. The sight made Sven's mouth water; he had eaten nothing all day, and was ravenously hungry. He thought of the miller and his wife, and wished he was back with them, sharing their evening meal. 'What fool's errand am I on?' he asked himself. . . . And then he thought of his mother, of her tears and her loneliness, and remembered that he had still to fight and kill the Dragon Troll who had carried his father away; and how the sword with which he could kill the Troll was somewhere within this great grim castle, and that it was up to him to get that sword. 'Keep a brave heart,' King Bear had said. Yes, yes, Sven would keep a brave heart. . .!

The sun had set, clouds gathered in a twilit sky, with now and then a pale star peeping out between the clouds. Sven could hear a great racket going on inside the castle, as the watchmen went their round locking up the doors. Then the great grim entrance door was flung open, and the watchmen came out, searching this way, searching that way.

'Anyone about?' called one watchman to another.

'No, nobody,' answered the other, passing so close to the invisible Sven, that Sven felt tempted to put out a foot and trip him up. . . .

But no. Sven must remember that he has other, and more important, work on hand. And the great entrance door is wide open. Quick, Sven, now is your chance! He is up the steps before the door, and in through the door in a twinkling. Where is he now? In a lofty hall, and round the hall on seven mats lie seven huge dogs.

Sniff, sniff, sniff! The dogs are up on their feet, snuffling and growling. But they cannot see Sven, and he passes by them. At the back of the hall is an alcove, and on the wall in the alcove hangs the sword that will kill the Dragon Troll: the sword that Sven has come all this way to fetch.

Sven puts up his hand to take down the sword. But it is so heavy that he cannot lift it. What can he do? He looks about him in dismay. He sees a table with three flasks of wine standing on it. The flasks are labelled. On one label is written, *'Seven men's strength.'*

Ah, with seven men's strength Sven can surely lift that sword! He takes up the flask and drinks the wine. The wine warms him through and through. He puts up his hand to the sword. No, he cannot lift it. He reads the label on the second flask of wine: *'Twenty men's strength.'* Eagerly he drinks down the wine from that second flask, and again puts up his hand to the sword. Now he can lift it down, but it takes all his strength to do so – and how can he use in the coming fight a weapon so heavy? He reads the label on the third flask: *'Thirty men's strength.'* He drops the sword, snatches up this third flask, puts it to his lips, empties it in one long gulp, and such strength flows through him as surely only a giant can possess! He takes up the sword, it feels like a straw in his hand, he whirls it round his head: dragons, demons, trolls – pah! Sven now feels he can defy you all!

Away then, Sven, away from this accursed castle of Trolls: away to find your father, and rescue the princess!

But as he is eagerly hurrying out of the castle, still invisible, and of course the sword he is holding being invisible too – the sword strikes against the alcove wall with a loud rattle. And immediately the air is filled with screams and howls and the trampling of feet, as out of many doors flung violently open, and down the great staircase, a host of Trolls come rushing. The seven dogs leap up from their seven mats and add to the din with their ferocious barking. But Sven is still wearing the glove, he is still invisible: he dodges between the crowd of yelling Trolls and barking dogs, and gets safely out of the palace.

'Phew, that was enough to turn a fellow's hair grey!' he said to himself, as he hurried away from the castle and back into the forest.

King Bear was waiting for him. 'Ah, you have the sword,' he said when he saw Sven. 'Well done, my lad! I have some food here for you, for I'm sure you must be hungry. But eat quickly now, and then be off with you back to Dragon Island. You have still to fight the Troll and rescue your father. . . And also someone else,' he added with a chuckle.

'And who is that?' said Sven.

'Bless the lad!' laughed King Bear. 'Why the very person you left the miller's house to seek. And now it seems you have forgotten all about her!'

The princess! Yes, indeed, in his anxiety about his father, Sven hadn't given her a thought. Now he remembered his dream, and how he had seen her shut up in a cellar, shedding bitter tears.

'It is the Troll who keeps her captive in that cellar,' said King Bear. . . . 'She will make you a charming wife, Sven.'

Sven laughed. *He* to marry a princess, a princess who would one day become a queen! And then what would Sven be? Prince Sven? Or even King Sven! Well, why not? Sven held his head high. He felt no end of a fine fellow, as he walked back through the forest to the shore of the great sea.

When he reached the sea, he pressed the fish scale between the palms of his hands. And the sea rose in a great white wave, and in the wave the Merman came swimming. The Merman carried Sven over to Dragon Island. And there Sven put on the glove that made him invisible, crept under the elder bush, and soon fell asleep.

6. Happy Ending

Meanwhile in his palace on the island, the Dragon Troll was holding council with his twelve sons.

'I have had a bad dream,' said the Dragon Troll. 'I dreamed that Sven had somehow managed to get hold of the magic sword, and had returned here to fight and kill me.' The Troll was really frightened. Truly he was a coward at heart. He was all a-quiver with anxiety, and the golden crowns on his three heads were shaking and flashing in the light of the many lamps that lit up the hall in which he and his twelve sons were sitting.

'Bah!' said one of the crow sons. 'If the miserable little creature has come here, we will set on him and peck his eyes out!'

Then the Troll's twelve sons turned into twelve crows. And the twelve crows hurried out, and went flying this way and that way over the island in search of Sven. But, he being invisible, of course they couldn't find him.

But Sven was up and on the alert, the magic sword unsheathed in his hand. He met the Dragon Troll in the middle of the island, and immediately gave battle. The Dragon Troll was roaring with rage, he was lashing the ground with his tail, causing the earth to thunder, and the whole island to tremble. But Sven struck out boldly with the magic sword, wounding the dragon here, wounding him there. *Chop!* Off went one of the Dragon's heads. *Chop!* Off went another head. Now the Dragon Troll was howling for mercy – what did Sven want of him? He would give Sven anything he asked for – anything, anything!

'All I want,' shouted Sven,' is that last head of yours!'

Chop! went the magic sword again. And the Dragon Troll's third head fell from his body.

'Hurrah!' shouted Sven in wild excitement. He hurried to the Troll's palace, where all the doors now stood open. And on the steps before the palace stood a lean, weary-looking old man.

'The Dragon Troll is dead!' shouted Sven. 'I, Sven, have killed him! Cheer up, old man, whoever you may be!'

'Sven?' faltered the lean, weary-looking old man. '*Sven?*'

'That is my name,' said Sven. He gave a startled glance at the old man. 'Can it be that – that you are my father?' he said.

'Yes, yes, Sven,' answered the man, 'your unhappy father, who sold his son for a never-empty purse, and has lived to regret it – oh how bitterly!'

'Father,' said Sven, 'there shall be no more regrets. It is time for counsel. We have still the Troll's twelve sons to deal with.'

Sven's father pursed up his lips into a bitter smile. 'I have already dealt with them,' he said. 'I poisoned the meat that I cooked for their dinner.

63

They all lie lifeless on the floor in the dining hall. Oh, I have taken my revenge on them, even though I believed that the Dragon Troll would tear me to pieces for it. And now the Troll himself is dead! Oh my son, my brave son!'

And the old man knelt and kissed Sven's feet.

'Nay,' said Sven, 'indeed we can't have this! Rise up, rise up – you put me to shame! And we have still to deliver the princess. Tell me, where is she?'

'I will bring you to where she is,' said Sven's father.

And he led Sven down into a cellar, where a lovely little princess sat weeping on a three-legged stool.

At the opening of the cellar door, the princess sprang to her feet. 'I will not, I will *not*!' she cried. 'You shall kill me first!' Then she gazed at Sven in bewilderment. 'Who – who are you?' she faltered. 'I – I thought it was the Troll.'

'The Troll is dead,' said Sven. 'I have fought and killed him. And all his sons are also dead, poisoned by this old gentleman who is my father. And now, most gracious princess, I have come to take you home.'

'Oh how beautiful she is, how beautiful!' Sven said to himself, as he took her gently by the hand and led her up out of the cellar. Indeed his heart was throbbing with love and pity. 'Come,' he said, 'we must lose no time in leaving this accursed island!'

So, hand in hand, Sven and the princess went down to the sea shore, with Sven's father walking beside them. And there Sven rubbed the fish scale between the palms of his hands. Then rose the great white wave; and in the wave came the Merman.

'At your command, my lord,' said the Merman.

'I wish for a boat to carry us to the mainland,' said Sven.

The Merman gave a shrill whistle. Hey presto! there was the boat. Sven and Sven's father and the princess got into the boat, and the Merman swam beneath it, and carried it swiftly, swiftly, over the waves to the mainland.

So our story comes to its end. Of course Sven married the princess. King Bear and little Mouse came to the wedding. And when the old king, the princess's father, died, the princess became queen, and Sven became king. As for Sven's father and mother, their days were now all gladness. Sven gave them back the never-empty purse, though Sven's father protested that he didn't deserve it. And Sven sent for the miller and offered him a dukedom.

But the miller said, 'Nay, nay, we are but humble folk. What should we do with a thing the like of that? It is enough for us to know that our dear adopted son is well and happy.'

And Sven *was* happy. With his beautiful and beloved queen he lived in happiness for all the rest of his life.

5. White Doviekin

1. The Interrupted Wedding

This is a story about Lord Terkild, and about his beautiful daughter Katrina, and young Prince Eric, and old witch Grab, and her stupid son Swip.

Katrina and Prince Eric loved each other dearly, and of course they wanted to get married. Katrina's father, Lord Terkild, was pleased that they should do so, and he arranged for a magnificent wedding. But old witch Grab was furious, because she wanted Katrina to marry her stupid son, Swip.

Well, the wedding day came. A sumptuous wedding breakfast was prepared for more than a hundred guests, the church bells were ringing a merry peal, the bridesmaids were fluttering about like a flock of chirruping birds. Now Katrina, in her beautiful white bridal robe and her bridal veil, was being led by her father up to the open church door, where the priest was waiting to welcome her, when – alack, alack! – old witch Grab, in the shape of a falcon, flew down with a shriek from the church tower, perched on Katrina's head and changed her into a white dove. And the white dove spread her wings and flew away, with the falcon close behind her, screaming, pecking, chasing her on and on.

Far away, far away flew the white dove, over fields and woods, over towns and villages; and still the falcon, on its long, swift wings, chased after her, pulling out the dove's feathers with its sharp, curved beak, and screaming, screaming.

And on they flew, and on.

Now they were flying through a clearing in the middle of a forest. In the clearing was a small house, and at an open window a little girl sat darning her father's socks. At her last gasp, the white dove flew in through the window, and fell into the little girl's lap.

'Oh, you poor darling white doviekin!' cried the little girl. Then she saw the falcon, and clasping the dove to her breast with one hand, she jumped up. 'Be off with you, you speckled devil!' she shouted. And with her free hand she made the sign of the Cross.

No evil thing can stand against that sign: the falcon-witch gave a scream, and flew swiftly away.

Then the little girl, still holding the dove close, fetched water and a spoon, and dripped the water into the white dove's beak.

'You shall stay with me, and I will take care of you, my doviekin,' she said. 'I will feed you on wild strawberries and sweet cream, and nothing shall hurt you, nothing shall frighten you. . . But you are tired, oh, so tired! Then put your head under your wing, my doviekin, and I will sing you to sleep.'

Then the poor weary dove put her head under her wing, and fell asleep on the little girl's lap.

By and by the little girl's father and mother came in, and also her big brother. They had all been out working in the fields beyond the forest. The little girl put her finger to her lips, and whispered 'Hush! See what a darling doviekin I have saved from a cruel falcon! I may keep it, mayn't I?'

'Yes, of course you can keep it,' said the little girl's mother.

So for a while, Katrina, Lord Terkild's lovely daughter, in the shape of a white dove, lived peacefully in the peasant's cottage.

But only for a little while; for old witch Grab was still determined that the lovely Katrina should marry her stupid son, Swip. So what did the

old witch do? She changed herself into a snake. And one day, when the white dove was alone in the cottage (the little girl being out with her father and mother and her big brother, working in the fields) old witch Grab in the shape of a big snake came crawling down the chimney into the peasant's cottage.

The poor little white dove was very frightened. She flew up on to a ceiling beam; and there she perched, and there she shuddered.

'Little white dove,' hissed the Snake, 'I have sad news for you. Your lover, Prince Eric, has wearied of waiting for you. He is courting another maiden, a princess more beautiful, and far more rich, than you are. But there is Madame Grab's son, the young and handsome Swip, so devoted, so true, breaking his heart for love of you. Now you must put all thoughts of Prince Eric out of your mind, and agree to marry the handsome Swip.'

'I do not believe you!' cried the little white dove. 'I will not, I will not, I will *not* marry anyone but my dear, dear Prince Eric!'

'Then you shall die!' hissed the Snake.

'If I am to die, yet I will remain true to my love, Prince Eric,' cried the little white dove.

The Snake hissed, the Snake writhed, the Snake was furious. But she did not really want to kill the white dove. What she wished was that the dove Katrina should marry her stupid son, Swip. For Katrina's father, Lord Terkild, was very rich, and witch Grab had a wicked plan in her head to cause Lord Terkild's death by her magic powers. And then, ah then, all Lord Terkild's great possessions would belong to Katrina, the little white dove, and the man whom Katrina married would live in clover.

'I'm not beaten yet,' said the snake-witch Grab to herself, as she crawled away.

So the next time that the little white dove was left alone, old witch Grab paid her another visit: this time in the shape of a huge black cat.

'Mi – ow,' said the huge black cat. 'I know who you are, little white dove. You are no more a dove than I am. You are Katrina, Lord Terkild's lovely daughter. I am clever, I am wise, I am a reader of destinies. And *your* destiny, young proud heart, is to wed with witch Grab's handsome son, young Swip. Do you agree?'

'No, I do *not*!' cried the little white dove.

'Then this is your last day!' snarled Cat Grab. 'For with my claws I will tear you to pieces!'

Then all the feathers on the little white dove's neck and back bristled and stood upright with anger. She flew at Cat Grab, and pecked her and pecked her. But Cat Grab fought back, feathers flew, fur flew, neither could overcome the other. And in the end Witch Grab turned into her own shape, scrambled out through the open window, and ran away, saying to herself, 'Who would have thought to find so true and valiant a heart in such a young girl!'

69

2. An Aviary Full of Doves

Now we must leave the little white dove, secure, if not entirely happy in the peasant's cottage, and go back to see what was happening in the home of Lord Terkild, her father. As you can well believe, there was trouble and turmoil enough in that home! The first thing that Lord Terkild did was to send a gang of horsemen galloping all over the country in search of the little white dove. And the foremost of those horsemen, you may be sure, was young Prince Eric, Katrina's lover. But in vain. For, as you will remember, the falcon had chased the white dove far away into a distant land; and though many a man had seen the beginning of the falcon's flight, no one had seen the end of it.

So, when Prince Eric, together with the other messengers, returned discomforted, Lord Terkild had another idea. He built a huge aviary, and let it be known that he wished to fill his aviary with white doves, and that he would pay a handsome price for any such doves as people would bring him. People brought him white doves in hundreds. And to each dove, before he put it into the aviary, Lord Terkild said, 'If you are my darling daughter, Katrina, speak to me! Or, if you cannot speak, nod your head and flutter your wings, and coo!'

Most of the white doves fluttered their wings, and some of them cooed, and one or two of them nodded their heads. But not one dove did all three of these things, and not one of them spoke. Yet Lord Terkild spent hours and hours sitting or standing outside the aviary, watching the doves, and hoping against hope that some day – any day – his dear daughter Katrina might come home to him.

Often Prince Eric, Katrina's lover, would come to sit beside Lord Terkild to watch the doves. And one day he said, 'Let us try singing to the doves. Perhaps one of them will understand and answer us.'

'Yes,' said Lord Terkild, 'let us try singing. You begin.'

So then the prince began to sing:

> 'White doviekin, white doviekin,
> Where are you, my sweet wifiekin?
> Be you not here, where are you then?
> If you be here, oh tell me then –
> White doviekin, white doviekin,
> Oh come my whitest wifiekin!'

But not one of the doves took any notice.

So then Katrina's father, Lord Terkild, began to sing:

> 'Cooroo, *my doviekin, cooroo!*
> *Cooroo, my swanikin, cooroo!*
> *If you still know me*
> *Your heart must burn you.*
> *Ah,* my *heart is burning all too sorely!*
> *Come, my white doviekin, if you are here!*'

But not one of the doves took any notice.

So days and weeks and months went by, and the aviary became full to overflowing. 'It is hopeless,' sighed Katrina's lover, Prince Eric. 'We shall never see Katrina again.'

But Katrina's father, Lord Terkild, would not give up hope. And now everybody was talking about this aviary of his, and of his demand for more doves. The news spread from town to town, and from village to village, all across the country, and at last came to the ears of the peasant family with whom the white dove now lived.

'Tis a handsome price that lord is offering,' said the peasant father. 'And times being hard, we could do with a bit more money.'

'You're right there,' said the peasant's wife.

'Oh no, no!' cried the peasant's little girl. 'I must keep my darling doviekin!'

'Well, I call that very selfish of you,' said the little girl's mother.

'And it's for me to decide, not you,' said her father.

The little girl shed tears; but at last she agreed to let her doviekin go to the aviary, provided that she might take it there herself. 'And I shall ask my lord Terkild to take me on as a dove-minder,' she said, 'for where my doviekin goes, I shall go.'

'You'll do nothing of the sort!' said her mother.

'All right then,' said the little girl defiantly, 'my doviekin and I will run away, and you'll never see either of us again.'

The little girl meant what she said, and her parents knew she meant it. So the peasant borrowed a donkey and cart: the peasant's wife packed up some food for the journey; the little girl took the white dove in her arms and clambered into the cart; the peasant whipped up the donkey, and they set off on their long journey to Lord Terkild's home.

When they reached Lord Terkild's great house, the peasant lifted the little girl down from the cart, looped the donkey's reins over a post by the entrance gate, took the little girl by the hand, and led her, still clasping the dove, round to the back of the great house, where they found Lord Terkild sitting unhappily in front of his aviary, that resounded with the cooing of the doves and the fluttering of their wings.

The peasant bobbed his head and touched his forelock. 'If you please my lord, we've brought you – '

But what was this? The white dove had struggled out of the little girl's arms. Straight, straight it flew to Lord Terkild, fluttering its wings against his breast, and cooing joyfully.

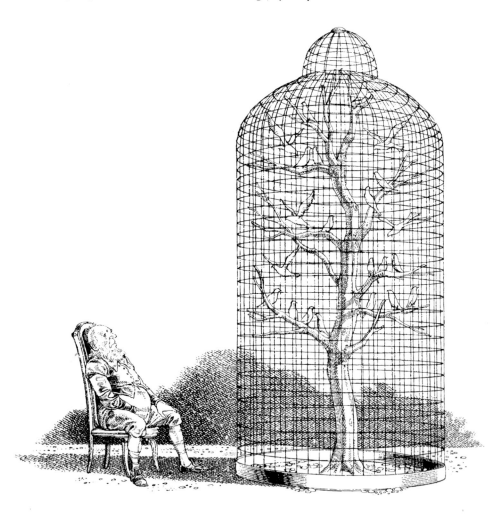

'Kiss me, kiss me, my dear father!' the white dove was saying.

Lord Terkild didn't understand what the white dove was saying, but he stroked its white feathers gently, and laid his cheek against it, and kissed it, murmuring the while, 'Oh pretty little dove, if only you were my long lost daughter, my dear, my lovely, my beloved Katrina!'

'But I am Katrina!' cried the dove.

And, see now, who was it that Lord Terkild held in his arms? No white dove, but his own darling Katrina!

Joy, joy, joy! Laughter instead of tears, happiness instead of misery – Katrina, released from her father's arms to fling herself into the arms of her lover, Prince Eric; the peasant receiving such a sum of money as would keep him and his wife in comfort for many a long day; the bells in the tower of Lord Terkild's great house ringing out merry peal after merry peal, everyone rejoicing, except the peasant's little girl, who has crept behind the aviary, and is sobbing.

'Oh my doviekin, my darling, darling doviekin,' sobs the little girl. 'What am I going to do without you?'

It is Katrina who misses the little girl; it is Katrina who sends to look for her, it is Katrina who takes her by the hand, and leads her, still sobbing, to Lord Terkild.

'Father,' said Katrina, 'this is my dear little friend, who has looked after me so tenderly through all these unhappy months. She has fed me, and caressed me, and indeed she has made these months not unhappy ones, but happy ones for me. I do not want to part with her. So please will you let her stay here, to be my comforter and playmate still?'

'Of course she shall stay, if that is your wish,' said Lord Terkild. 'We will feed her and clothe her, and when she is a little older she shall be paid a good wage as your lady-in-waiting. That is, if her father is agreeable?'

The little girl's father was agreeable. He went home to his wife with a bagful of gold coins, and the news that their little daughter was 'made for life' as he expressed it. 'And you needn't pull that long face, old woman,' he said, 'because we can pay the little rascal a visit whenever we've a mind to. I have my lord's promise for bed and board, and everything handsome.'

So then the little girl's mother cheered up, and said that she supposed everything had worked out for the best.

But there was someone for whom everything was not working out for the best, and that was the witch. She was champing and stamping and

73

screaming with rage. Lord Terkild sent officers to arrest her. But before they could reach her, she changed herself and her stupid son, Swip, into black ravens. The ravens spread their wings and flew far, far away. Nor were they ever seen on earth again.

Now came the wedding of Katrina and Prince Eric. And, after the wedding, Lord Terkild gave a feast to all his people. The feast was followed by a dance, with fiddlers and harpists and pipers and trumpeters to make merry music. And as the people danced they sang.

This was their song:

> 'White doviekin, white doviekin,
> Oh what a lovely loviekin,
> Prince Eric's darling wifiekin.'

6. *The Barrel Man*

Once upon a time there was a lad called Tonda, who earned his living by making birch brooms and selling them in the market. Well, he didn't earn much that way, and indeed he was very poor. But he was a good lad, and a merry lad, and everyone liked him. So from one woman it would be, 'Tonda, take off that ragged coat of yours, and I'll put a patch on it for you.' And from another woman, 'Tonda, I've a bit of stew in the pot, if so be you'd like a plateful.' And from one man or another it would be, 'Tonda, young fellow, what about the tavern and a glass of beer?'

So Tonda did well enough. He thought the world was a very pleasant place, and he never worried about anything.

Well, one day in the tavern the men were all talking about a rich baron who had come into town seeking a servant. And to such a man as suited him he was offering to give twenty pounds a month, beside bed, board, and an outfit of clothes.

Now when Tonda heard this news he had but twenty pence in his pocket, and that was all he had in the world. So he jumped up and said, 'That's the place for me!'

And off with him to the house where the Baron was lodging, to offer his services.

The Baron had a haughty way with him. He hummed and hawed, and looked Tonda up and down, as if he couldn't make up his mind. But at last he said, 'Very well, you may consider yourself engaged. But mind you, from this hour my will shall be yours.'

'In all things just and right I will obey you,' said Tonda, who wasn't quite sure that he liked the look in the Baron's eyes.

'Bah!' said the Baron. 'And who is to decide what is just and right – you or I?'

'Well, both of us, I suppose,' said Tonda.

'Bah!' said the Baron again. Then he told Tonda to go to the nearby stables, and saddle and bridle two horses he would find there. And when Tonda had done this, he and the Baron rode off together.

After a short ride they came to the Baron's mansion, where there were plenty of other servants. Tonda, indeed had little to do but to feed and groom the two horses, and to ride them out in turn to exercise them. Sometimes, too, he drove with the Baron in a gaudy little carriage. On these occasions he wore a green livery and felt very smart. But he wasn't exactly happy. The other servants were a stiff melancholy lot. They went about with pursed up lips and downcast eyes. It seemed to Tonda that not one of them was willing to look him in the face. He sorely missed the friendly company in the town he had left. And when he had been with his new master for a month, he said to himself, 'Well now, I have earned twenty pounds, and yet if I ask for a glass of beer, I can't have it! And as for a merry laugh – it seems that I can't have that, either. How would it be if I just took a walk back to town, and had a chat with some of my old friends in the tavern? Yes, that I'll do!'

Well, he was just setting off when a maidservant came running after him to say that he must come back quickly, because he had to ride out with the Baron.

'Blast the Baron!' said Tonda. 'Can't a fellow do as he pleases for half an hour or so?'

'Not with a master such as ours, you can't,' said the maidservant.

Then she went back into the house. And Tonda stamped off to the stables, and saddled and bridled the two horses.

Very soon the Baron came out. He was bringing an enormous sack, which he bade Tonda to roll up and place before him on his saddle bow. 'I have some heavy purchases to make and bring home,' he said.

'Yes, but – ' said Tonda. 'Shan't we need another horse to carry the purchases home?'

'Bah!' said the Baron. 'Mind your own business!'

Then he leaped on to one of the horses, and bidding Tonda mount the other and follow him, he set off at a hard gallop, up hill and down dale, till they came to the sea, and down over the sands to the edge of the water.

'*Well*,' thought Tonda. 'Here's craziness! We can't go any farther this way.'

But what was the Baron doing? First he was riding a little way into the water; then he was leaning from the saddle and striking the water with his whip. And – well, what do you think? The water drew back on either side, rearing up like two great walls, and between the walls of water there appeared a wide pathway, stretching on and on as far as the eye could see.

Along this pathway galloped the Baron; and along the pathway galloped Tonda after him. But Tonda wasn't liking it – no he was *not!* To be the servant of such a man as this didn't seem right or natural. Better perhaps to go back to the town, and take up his old trade of broom-binding?

And so thinking, he turned to look round.

Oh worse and worse! The waters of the sea had closed up behind them. They were in the midst of a great ocean. There was nothing for it but to follow the Baron, and ride on.

So they rode, rode, rode; and came at last to another country and another shore. And on a plateau not far from the sea stood a great black castle. There was not a human being to be seen; but round the pinnacled roofs of the castle, a flock of white pigeons was fluttering and cooing.

The Baron, with Tonda following, rode up to the castle.

'Tonda,' said the Baron, 'you see that ladder lying on the ground, and you see that open window?'

'Yes, I see them,' said Tonda.

'Then get down from your horse,' said the Baron. 'Set the ladder up against the window. Climb up the ladder and go in through the window. Throw all the money you find inside there down to me. And hurry, hurry! I don't intent to wait here all day!'

Tonda hesitated. But the Baron snatched a pistol from his belt, and levelled it at Tonda's head. 'Do as you're told,' he snarled. 'or you're a dead man!'

So then Tonda set the ladder against the wall, and climbed up, and stepped in through the window. Now he was in a little room, and all round the room there were piles of glittering gold pieces. Tonda hadn't decided what to do next. But one thing he *had* decided – he was not going to steal anybody's money! Perhaps he might shout a warning to whomsoever lived in the castle? Yes, that would be best!

But it seemed to him that the room was growing dark: and glancing at the window, he saw that it was getting smaller and smaller. Indeed every moment that window was narrowing! He ran to it and looked out. Down below the Baron was calling, 'Hey, Tonda, throw down the money. Throw it down!'

'*No*,' shouted Tonda, 'I can't and I won't! If I can get myself out of here, it's as much as I can do!'

Truly he was caught in a trap! Even as he shouted those last words the window narrowed itself to a mere thread. Next moment the window was gone. And Tonda was left in the dark.

'Hi! hi! hi!' Now he was shouting and banging on the walls. Then his shouting was swallowed up in a monstrous rattling din, like continuous thunder; a door opened and there came rolling towards him a huge black barrel, all lit up by some light of its own. The barrel rolled as far as Tonda's feet. Then it burst into two parts, and out of it stepped a man who was glowing red from head to foot like a great ruby.

'Tonda, Tonda,' roared the Barrel Man, 'what are you doing here?'

'Oh sir, oh sir,' cried Tonda, 'indeed I don't know. But I haven't handed out a single penny, nor did I mean to!'

'Then what are you doing here?' roared the Barrel Man again.

'I – I was sent,' stammered Tonda, feeling very frightened and very foolish. 'I was – obeying the orders of my master.'

'Those who obey the wicked come to grief,' said the Barrel Man. 'Follow me.'

And he led Tonda through the door and into a long gallery, lit by many windows. The Barrel Man opened one of the windows, and bade Tonda look out. 'What do you see down there, Tonda?'

'Bones,' said Tonda. 'Bones and skulls and – and – '

'Those are the bones of the servants your master has sent to perish here,' said the Barrel Man. 'There have already been ninety-nine of them. Were you to have been the hundredth, Tonda?'

'That's as may be,' said Tonda. 'I don't know. But one thing I do know. I'm no thief!' Now he was feeling angry. 'Do you think I'm lying when I tell you that I was about to raise the alarm, when you made that window shut on me and caught me in a trap?'

The Barrel Man looked at Tonda with eyes that seemed to pierce him through and through. 'No, Tonda,' he said at last, 'I do not think you are lying. Come now, we will be friends, and you shall stay here and serve me.'

'If I must, I must,' said Tonda, not too willingly. Because, after all, a man who leaped out of a glowing barrel, and that man ruby red, was not the kind of master that anyone would expect to serve. He heartily wished he was back in his home town, making and selling his birch brooms. But since then he had crossed the sea, and he didn't know where in the world he now was.

'I have two mules and a nanny goat for you to look after,' said the Barrel Man.

On hearing that, Tonda cheered up. He was very fond of animals.

Then the Barrel Man led Tonda along many corridors, and up and down many staircases, and he brought him out of the castle into a meadow, where a little white nanny goat and two mules were peacefully grazing. When the two mules saw the Barrel Man they whinnied and came trotting up to him. As for the little nanny goat, she lifted her head and stared at Tonda for a while. Then she too came running. And what did she do but lay her head in Tonda's hand, and look up into his face with eyes which Tonda could almost swear were full of tears.

And Tonda stroked her head and said, 'All right, all right, little lady! Nothing to worry about. I'm going to be good to you – see if I'm not!'

Then the Barrel Man took Tonda to the stables, and showed him where the corn and the hay and the currycomb and brushes were kept. He told Tonda that he must groom the animals every day, and also give

79

them one good feed of corn every morning and see that their water trough was full, but that he needn't bother to stable them, because they could please themselves about being in the stable or out of it. 'And now, Tonda,' he said as they went back into the castle, 'I am going to leave you. I will see you again a month from today.'

Then came again a flash of lightning and a peal of thunder; and the huge black barrel came rolling in and burst into two parts. The Barrel Man stepped into the barrel, the barrel closed itself, and rolled away.

'*Well!*' said Tonda, 'I'll be hanged if I know what to make of all this! But one thing I do know – I'm hungry!'

And no sooner had he said 'I'm hungry' than hey presto! a table appeared spread with all kinds of good food: soup, meat, puddings, and a flagon of wine. So Tonda sat down and ate and drank. And after that he went out and talked to the mules and the nanny goat, and came in again, and wandered through the castle, and found a room with a bed made up in it, and also everything he might want in the way of brush and comb and nightshirt and toothbrush and soap and washing water. So, being very tired, he undressed, got into bed, and slept soundly till next morning.

In the morning he woke feeling fit as a fiddle. And having washed and dressed, he found he had only to go into the room where he had supped, and say 'I should like my breakfast,' when that breakfast appeared, with a bowl of porridge, and eggs and bacon, and sausages and toast.

'A breakfast fit for a king!' said Tonda. 'But I wish I had someone to talk to!'

No good wishing for that, it seemed, for nobody came. And though he spoke that wish out loud many times whilst eating his breakfast, still nobody came. So, when he had finished breakfast, he went out and fed and groomed the two mules and brushed the nanny goat's white hair. And then he rode the mules in turn through the meadows and down along the shore of the great sea. And each time he came back into the field, there was the nanny goat running up to lay her head in his hand, and look at him with loving eyes.

'If you could speak, my lady,' said Tonda, 'I think you'd have a strange tale to tell me.'

And then the nanny goat gave a little whimpering bleat, as if to say, 'Oh, how I wish I *could* speak to you!'

So the days passed. And though Tonda wasn't exactly happy, he wasn't exactly unhappy. Only he did so long to have someone to talk to, other than the mules and the nanny goat. For he was sociable fellow, and fond of company.

'I wish, oh I wish I had something to amuse me!' he said one day after dinner in the room where he got his meals.

What happened? Hey presto! Down on to the table fell a pack of cards!

Then Tonda was really angry. He swept the cards off the table on to the floor. He was stamping on them and calling them names, when there came a flash of lightning and a clap of thunder, and into the room rolled the black barrel, all lit up with its own peculiar brilliance. The barrel broke in two; and out from it stepped the Barrel Man.

'Well, Tonda,' said the Barrel Man, 'and how are you getting on? I see that you have everything in good order here, and that pleases me.'

'But it doesn't please *me!*' cried Tonda. 'I'm so lonely that I could howl like a dog! I ask for something to amuse me – and what do I get? A pack of cards! It's company I want, company I tell you! Do you want me to go mad here all by myself?'

'Go mad?' said the Barrel Man. 'Nay, nay, Tonda, that will never do! You shall have company. And yet, and yet, I don't know. May hap it will turn out badly for us all.'

'All!' shouted Tonda, thoroughly beside himself. 'Who are your "*all*," and what do I care about them? Let me go back to my own native town, let me bind brooms and be beggarly poor, and – and – '

Now there was Tonda with his head on the table, sobbing as if his heart would break.

'Tonda,' said the Barrel Man. 'You are a good lad, and I believe you are a brave lad, and I am going to trust you as I have never yet trusted anyone in my life. Come with me.'

Then the Barrel Man led Tonda out of the castle and pointed to a path that wound its way through a little wood. 'Go into that wood, Tonda,' he said, 'and walk on until you come to a lake. It is in the waters of that lake that you will find your company. Here is a cap for you to wear. With this cap on your head, you will be able to breathe freely under the water. Oh Tonda, Tonda, if you will be but faithful and brave and true, you will bring such a blessing on me and on all those who are dear to me, as will make me your debtor for life!'

Then the Barrel Man went back into the castle. And Tonda, greatly wondering, went on into the wood and through the wood, and came out into a valley surrounded by small grassy hills. In the valley was a lake of bright water, and as Tonda drew near he saw a white pigeon rise out of the lake, shake the water drops from its wings and fly up into the sky. Next moment another white pigeon rose out of the lake and followed the first one, and then a third pigeon, and a fourth and a fifth and a sixth – a whole flock of pigeons rising one after the other, and shaking the water from their wings, and flying up, up, and out of sight.

Well, well, Tonda wasn't going to be beaten by a flock of pigeons! If they could rise out of the lake, he could go down into it; without hesitating for a moment, he put the cap the Barrel Man had given him on to his head, and plunged into the water.

Down he went, deep, deep down, and coming to the bottom – what did he find there? What but a palace whose glassy walls gleamed and glittered with a silvery light. He went into the palace, and through one room and through another room, and came into a small bright parlour, where a beautiful young girl sat at an open window. The girl had a white staff in one hand and a knife in the other hand. She was whittling little slices off the staff; and as each slice fell to the ground it turned into a white pigeon, flew out of the open window, and rose up through the lake like a bubble.

When the young girl saw Tonda she was frightened, and jumped up as if to run from the room. But Tonda said, 'Please, *please* don't run away! Please stay and talk to me! It was the Barrel Man who sent me, because I was so lonely.'

'Oh,' said the girl, 'you can't be more lonely that I am! And if my father sent you, I welcome you gladly.'

So Tonda sat down beside her, and they talked together. The girl told him that her name was Lexandra, and that her father was a king, enchanted by a wizard because he would not give her to that wizard as a bride. The wizard had turned her mother, the queen, into a nanny goat, and her two brothers into mules.

'And my dear father put me down into this pool so that the Wizard shouldn't reach me,' said Lexandra, 'because he is a fire Wizard and may not venture into water. Now and then my father comes to visit me. And meanwhile I send my pigeons to fly round the castle as a sign that all is well with me. My father has told me all about you, and how good you are. And so, Tonda, I have been longing to see you. . . And now you are here!' she said smiling at him.

'Yes, now I am here,' said Tonda. 'But what comes next?'

'Indeed I don't know,' said the princess. 'You must ask my father.'

So they chatted together for an hour or more. And when Tonda said goodbye to the princess, and went up through the water and back to the castle, he was deeply in love for the first time in his life.

'If I can kill that Wizard and set them all free, I will do it,' he told himself. 'And if I cannot kill the Wizard, I can but die in the attempt.'

The Barrel Man was in the meadow, talking to the mules and the nanny goat. 'Well, Tonda,' he said, 'did you find a pleasant companion?'

'Oh sir,' said Tonda, 'I found your daughter, and she told me about everything. And indeed you must forgive me if I have ever grumbled! For what are my troubles compared to yours? If you will give me a sword and direct my way, I will set out and fight this accursed Wizard. I will not lie down in a bed again, until I have made an end of him, or he has made an end of me!'

'I will give you a sword,' said the Barrel Man, 'and I will give you also something much more useful. Take this ring. You have but to turn it once on your finger and it will carry you to any place you may wish to go. You have but to turn it twice on your finger, and it will change you into any shape you may desire of it. You have but to turn it three times on your finger, and it will bring you back here to us.'

'If I live to come back,' said Tonda.

'That is as Heaven wills,' said the Barrel Man. 'And who can read the decrees of Heaven? But at least you go with my blessing.'

So Tonda buckled on the sword, and put the ring on his finger. Then, having patted the two mules, and stroked the nanny goat's little white head, and shaken the Barrel Man's hand, he turned the ring once, and wished to go to the place where he might find the Wizard. Immediately he was lifted off his feet and carried high into the air, with the wind whistling through his hair, and the earth, with its seas and rivers, fields, towns, forests, plains and mountains, seeming to rush backward beneath him at a dizzying pace.

And then – *bump!* He was standing on his feet again. He had come to the end of his journey. Where was he? On the top of a high hill of smooth grass. Behind the hill was a sycamore wood, and at the bottom of the hill was a rapidly running river.

Tonda had scarcely time to take a look at his surroundings, when out of the wood flew a Raven, screaming pitifully.

'My baby, my baby, my one last darling baby!' screamed the Raven. 'Oh, oh, he has fallen out of the nest! The Wizard has eaten his father, the Wizard has eaten all the rest of my children, and now he will eat this one, who is all, all I have left in the world! On the nest I can cover him with my wings and protect him. But I cannot, I cannot protect him when he lies on the ground!'

'Show me where he lies,' said Tonda. 'I will put him back in the nest for you.'

Then Tonda followed the Raven into the wood, and found the fledgeling on the ground under a sycamore tree. It was gasping and squawking, with its beak so wide open that Tonda could see all down its bright red throat. It didn't take long for Tonda to pick it up, and climb the tree, and put it back in the nest again. And then the Raven got into the nest also, and spread her wings over the little one, and said, 'I will never forget this, Tonda, never, never. Perhaps the time will come when I can repay you!'

But Tonda laughed and said, 'It was a very little thing to do, my Raven. And surely I need no repayment.'

Then he heard a loud shouting, and hurried out of the wood again.

There stood the Wizard, tall, lean, hideous, thin-lipped, bald-headed, with eyes like burning coals.

'So you have come to meet your death, Tonda,' sneered the Wizard.

'Or for you to meet yours,' said Tonda.

And he drew his sword.

The Wizard snapped his fingers. Now he too had a sword. They rushed upon one another. That was a fight! For one hour they fought, for two hours, for three. And over their heads hovered the Raven anxiously watching. Tonda had never handled a sword before. He knew no more how to use it than a baby. But it seemed the sword fought for him. At any rate it kept the Wizard at bay; and at the end of those three hours not one wound had been given or received.

So what did the Wizard do next? He changed himself into a red dragon. With flaming mouth wide open, that dragon rushed at Tonda. But Tonda turned the ring on his finger twice, and changed himself into a green dragon.

The two dragons came together, roaring, pouncing, snarling, biting, spitting out flames. But neither could overcome the other. And over their heads flew the Raven, anxiously watching.

For an hour they fought, but neither could overcome the other. So at the end of that hour the red dragon turned back into the Wizard; and Tonda, the green dragon, feeling that though he was determined to kill his enemy, he must at all costs fight fair, shook off his dragon shape also. Now Tonda and the Wizard stood glaring at one another. And then the Wizard laughed.

'I see that neither of us is going to destroy the other,' he said. 'So I propose a race. We will change ourselves into two wheels and roll down the hill. If the wheel that is myself reaches the bottom before the wheel that is you, you must consider yourself beaten and go your way. If the wheel that is you reaches the bottom before the wheel that is I, then I will consider myself beaten, and I will lift my spell from off the Black Castle and those that dwell therein. Is that agreed?'

'Yes, I suppose so,' said Tonda, rather unwillingly.

'Or of course,' sneered the Wizard, 'we can leave everything as it is – if that is more to your liking?

'No, no, no,' cried Tonda, 'anything but that!'

So standing on the top of the hill, each one turned himself into a wheel. The Wizard turned into a red wheel, Tonda turned into a green one. And the two wheels began to roll down the hill, fast, fast, faster – so fast that they became red hot, and likely at any moment to burst into flames.

And over the wheels hovered the Raven, anxiously watching.

'Raven, dear Raven,' called the red wheel, 'go down to the river, dip your beak and your wings into the water, and come and wet my rim!'

'Wizard, dear Wizard,' answered the Raven, 'have you forgotten who ate my babies and my beloved husband? Oh yes, certainly I will fetch water; but not for you!'

And she flew swiftly down to the river, and flew swiftly back again, to scatter water from her beak and her wet wings on to the rim of the green wheel that was Tonda.

And on down the hill rolled the wheels, fast, fast, faster. The red

wheel, that was the wizard, was now a sheet of flame, but the green wheel that was Tonda was cool and damp. Now they were nearing the river, and the flaming red wheel was well ahead of the green wheel. Was the Wizard going to win the race? Was Tonda to go back to the Black Castle an unhappy, defeated lad. . .? But see how the red wheel was burning, burning. The rim was afire, the spokes were afire, and just as it reached the river bank it burst into flaming fragments. The fragments fell into the river, and the river carried them away.

That was the end of the Wizard.

Then the green wheel turned back into Tonda. And Tonda said goodbye to the Raven, turned the ring on his finger, and wished himself back at the Black Castle. Now he was lifted off his feet and being whirled through the air so fast that the wind that was before him fell behind him, and the wind that was behind him could not catch up with him again.

But when he was set down on his feet once more, he found himself standing in the garden of a white palace, with roses and honeysuckle scenting the air, and birds singing among flowering bushes.

'I said the Black Castle,' said Tonda, turning the ring again.

The ring lifted him into the air a very, very little way – and set him down on his feet again.

'What's the matter with you?' cried Tonda irritably. 'Didn't you hear what I said? The Black Castle!'

Then he heard a laughing voice behind him.

'Tonda, dear Tonda, this *is* the Black Castle. Or it was the Black Castle until you turned it again into a white palace for us. Tonda, dear Tonda, welcome home!'

Tonda swung round. There was his princess, his lovely Lexandra, holding out her hands and tiptoeing to kiss him.

Then into the garden to greet him came a stately king and a gracious queen – the stately king who was but yesterday the Barrel Man, and the gracious queen who was but yesterday a little nanny goat. And following the king and queen came two young princes, who, believe it or not, were but yesterday two mules. It was so strange that Tonda thought he must be dreaming. But he was not dreaming, it was all real. For the Wizard was dead, and his wicked spells had died with him.

What more to tell? Only this – that of course Tonda married his princess. And though he was never heir to the throne, because the king had two sturdy sons, yet all the honours that could be heaped upon him were heaped upon him. And he, who only a short time ago had been but a humble broom-binder, became one of the greatest in the land.

So now farewell to you, Tonda, my lad! You have done valiantly. You have freed your friends and won your princess. And may you live happily with her ever after!

7. *Silver Hoof*

1. Koko Vanya and Gregoria

There was a woodcutter called Koko Vanya. Once he had a wife and three sons. But his wife had died, and his sons had grown up, and married and left him. Now he felt very lonely. So he thought, 'Well, why not adopt a child? A little girl would be best, because she would be useful about the house. Yes, that's what I will do. I will adopt a little girl.'

So he went to a friendly priest, and asked him if he knew of any little girl who would be thankful for a good home.

Yes, the priest knew of the very child. She was an orphan. Her name was Gregoria, and her father had made a foolish will. He had left his house and all his possessions to some cousins of his, on condition that they would live in his house with Gregoria, and take care of her until she grew up and married. Take care of the child indeed! Those cousins made a slave of her, and often beat her for nothing at all, except that they had lost their tempers.

'I am sure that Gregoria will be glad enough to come to you,' said the priest. 'And you are a good man. I know that you will be kind to her.'

'I should be wicked indeed if I were not kind to her,' said Koko Vanya. And he thanked the priest, and hurried away to little Gregoria's house.

Well well, what a little beauty that child was! Only much too thin and pale. Koko Vanya found her on her knees, scrubbing the kitchen floor, with no other companion but a big brown cat.

Koko Vanya told her that the priest had sent him, and asked her if she would like to come and live with him. And she jumped up, clapped her hands, and said, 'Oh yes, *please!*' Then she slipped her arm through his, and they went away together. And the big brown cat followed at their heels.

Well, it was a happy change for both Koko Vanya and little Gregoria. They had both been lonely, and now they both had someone to love. Koko Vanya whistled merrily over his wood-chopping in the forest; little Gregoria sang merry songs, instead of shedding tears, as she swept and dusted, and washed and mended Koko Vanya's clothes, and cooked the supper. And after supper they sat cosily by the kitchen fire and told each other fairy tales until bedtime. And the brown cat sat purring at their feet.

There was one story of Koko Vanya's that fascinated Gregoria. It was about a goat. This goat had a silver hoof, and when he stamped with this hoof, the ground became covered with diamonds and pearls and rubies and emeralds.

'Grandfather,' said little Gregoria, 'is the goat very big?'

'Oh no,' said Koko Vanya, 'he doesn't stand higher than our kitchen table, and he has a small head and pretty little slender legs.'

'Grandfather, has he got horns?'

'Oh yes, splendid horns. You know ordinary goats have only one prong to their horns, but he has five!'

'Grandfather, does he eat people?'

'Oh no,' laughed Koko Vanya. 'He doesn't harm anybody. He eats grass and leaves. Though in the winter he may perhaps steal a bit of hay from the stacks – but there, why not?'

'Grandfather, does he smell nasty?'

'I should say not,' said Koko Vanya, 'I expect he smells of the forest, and that's a pleasant smell. Though I have never been near enough to him to know about that. But it's time we both went to our beds, my girl. So no more stories until tomorrow evening. . .'

2. Silver Hoof

So for Koko Vanya and little Gregoria a happy summer followed a happy spring, and the happy summer was followed by a happy autumn. Then came the coldest winter that Koko Vanya could ever remember – snow thick on the ground, long icicles hanging on the leafless tree branches: a time when people were glad enough to get indoors, and crouch over blazing fires.

But Koko Vanya couldn't afford to sit all day by the fire. It was just the season when he could earn most, for you may be sure that pine logs were in great demand. And one day he said to Gregoria, 'Sweetheart, I must leave you for a while. It is impossible for me to go back and forth into the forest every day in this snow. Yet I must go on working lest we starve. I have a hut in a clearing among the trees, where I can light a fire and eat and sleep. You must stay here. You will be quite safe, for all the neighbours are friendly, and as you know, we have a good store of food.

'Oh *no*, Grandaddy,' cried Gregoria, 'let me come with you!'

'*Come with me!* My dear child, the forest in winter is no place for little girls.'

Gregoria didn't say another word. She shut her lips tight. But there was a determined look on her face which ought to have told Koko Vanya that she was not to be denied.

Next morning Koko Vanya got into his warmest coat, and his thickest boots, kissed Gregoria goodbye, and set off for the forest, dragging his sleigh behind him, his head bent against the bitter wind and still-falling snow. And as soon as he was out of sight – what did little Gregoria do? She too put on her warmest clothes (in fact she put on one dress on top of another), and tied a shawl round her shoulders.

'Pussy,' she said to the brown cat, 'don't you think it's a great shame, that you and I should be left alone like this?'

'*Mi-a-ow*, yes I do,' said the brown cat.

'Well then,' said little Gregoria, 'isn't there another sledge in the outhouse?'

'*Mi-a-ow*, yes there is,' said the brown cat.

'So this is what we'll do,' said little Gregoria, 'We'll load that sledge with blankets and food, and we'll go to join Grandaddy in the forest. Of course he may be a *little* cross, but he won't be cross long, because he'll really be glad to see us. And oh pussy, if we're lucky we may meet the goat with the silver hoof! Won't that be exciting?'

'Mi-a-ow-ow,' said pussy doubtfully. 'I'm not much interested in goats myself.'

'You'll be interested in this one, I promise you,' said Gregoria. And she hurried to make up a parcel of things to take with her. What should she take? A nightgown, a warm dressing jacket, a sponge, a brush and comb – oh botheration, that would have to do, she couldn't think of anything else. So having put on her warmest coat and her thickest boots, she hurried to the shed.

Now she is lifting the luggage into the sledge; now she is dragging the sledge out of the shed; now the brown cat has jumped up on top of the parcel; and now there is Gregoria ready to pull the sledge like any prancing pony. And now – hurrah! they are off.

Oh what a journey! Here and there the snow lay in great drifts across the path, and it was all Gregoria could do to drag the sledge over them. Now and then she slipped on a frozen puddle. Now and then she stumbled against a snow-hidden boulder. The cold north wind smote her in the face; and when she got into the forest, continual spatters of snow fell from the wind-tormented tree branches, and covered her from head to foot.

But still she plodded bravely on. And now – hurrah! She had come to a clearing where stood a big wooden hut. Through the window of the hut she could see the merry flicker of a welcoming fire; and there by the fire sat Koko Vanya, eating his dinner.

'Pussy, we've arrived!' said Gregoria. And she snatched her bundle off the sledge, and ran into the hut.

When Koko Vanya saw her – my word, he was angry! He called her a bad, wicked girl, and said other unkind things that made her cry.

But to make her cry was something new and very horrible to him. So he took her on his knees, and kissed and comforted her. He told her he was really glad she had come, for he had been feeling very lonely and out of spirits with nothing to do, as the weather was too bad for log-cutting. And he had just made a stew of wild fowl, and now she and the brown cat must help him to eat it. And of course now she had come, she must stay; he had plenty of blankets, and he would make up a bed for her on the floor in front of the fire.

'And have you seen little Silver Hoof, Grandaddy?' asked Gregoria.

'Yes, I saw him this very morning,' said Koko Vanya. 'He was snuffling round the hut, and I threw out some bread for him.'

'Oh Grandaddy, will he come again, do you think?'

'Maybe he will, maybe he won't,' said Koko Vanya. 'I expect it depends on how hungry he is.'

'Oh, I do hope he will be *very* hungry!' said Gregoria.

And Silver Hoof did come again. He came next morning. Koko Vanya was out log-cutting, and Gregoria was sitting by the fire with the brown cat on her knees, when Silver Hoof pushed the door open with his horns, and stepped into the room. Oh how beautiful, how very beautiful he was! Gregoria sat quite still, lest she should scare him, but her heart was thumping with excitement. Dare she get up and offer him a loaf of bread? Or would he rush away if she moved? But what had he come for? Surely he had come just for that – for food! So she got up softly softly, softly, softly opened a cupboard door, took down three bread rolls, and held them out to Silver Hoof.

Silver Hoof gobbled up one; he gobbled up another; he took the third in his mouth, and walked sedately out of the hut again.

'Pussy,' whispered little Gregoria, 'did you ever think that any animal in the world could be so beautiful?'

The brown cat thought there were many more beautiful animals in the world, and that one of them was now sitting at Gregoria's feet. And he told her so.

But Gregoria wasn't listening. She had gone to the door, and was peering out to see if she could get another glimpse of Silver Hoof. But she could see nothing except the tree branches swaying in the wind, with the snow dripping from them.

3. Present of Jewels

So through a month of bitter weather Gregoria lived with Koko Vanya in the forest hut, not able to put so much as her nose out of doors, but as happy as could be, cleaning, cooking, darning the holes in Koko Vanya's socks, mending the tears in his trousers, and above all looking forward to a daily visit from Silver Hoof, proud little Silver Hoof, who took food from her hand as if it were his right, and never deigned to show his gratitude.

And one evening Koko Vanya said, 'Gregoria, my darling, the road is clear, and I think we can manage to go home tomorrow.'

'O-oh,' said Gregoria, 'must we go? I do like it here so much, Grandaddy.'

Koko Vanya laughed. 'East, west, home's best,' he said.

But Gregoria rubbed her fist across her eyes. She was trying hard not to cry. 'If we go home perhaps I shall never see Silver Hoof again,' she was thinking. . .

That night Koko Vanya was wakened from his sleep by a curious noise on the roof of the hut. *Slap, bang, tinkle, tinkle, tinkle.* Someone must be up there! But who? Thieves? No surely not! Thieves move quietly, they do not make a noise. . . Besides there was nothing in his poor hut that a thief would think it worth while to steal. Should he take his gun and a lantern and go out to see what the noise was all about? Oh botheration, no! Why should he? It might be only two wild cats having a quarrel, or a couple of night hawks – with spring coming on they fought like furies over their mates. He yawned, pulled the blankets up round his chin, and fell asleep again.

Early next morning he woke to find Gregoria tugging at his sleeve. 'Grandaddy, oh Grandaddy, come out and *look!* There are bright glittering things lying all over the ground and a pile of them up on the roof. Oh Grandaddy, I think they must be jewels. . .!'

And they were jewels, heaps and heaps of jewels; pearls, rubies, emeralds, diamonds, sapphires, amethysts. Koko Vanya could scarcely believe his eyes – who could have brought them there – who – who?

'I think,' whispered Gregoria in an awed voice, 'it must be a present from Silver Hoof.'

And Gregoria was right – that's what it was. They saw him just for one instant, peeping at them from behind a tree, nodding his head as if to say, 'Yes, yes.' But before they could hurry to thank him, he was gone, nor did they ever see him again.

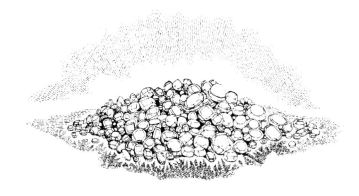

That day they went home with the two sledges piled high with jewels. Now from the sale of those jewels they were rich. Koko Vanya had no need to go again to the forest to chop down wood. But he did not intend to be idle. He bought a farm with many acres of surrounding fields, kept a large flock of sheep, some fine horses and a herd of cows. He hired men servants and maid servants, but he would not allow Gregoria to be idle either. She must learn to milk the cows, and make butter and cheese, and in such spare time as she had, he sent her to the kind old priest, who taught her to write neatly and to spell correctly, and to learn history and geography.

'For you are going to be a very rich young lady, my darling,' said Koko Vanya. 'And for a rich young lady to be ignorant would be a disgrace.'

So many happy years passed, and Gregoria grew from a pretty little girl into a beautiful young maiden, and fell in love and married. Can you guess whom she married? Yes, you're right, she married a prince.

But that is another story. And here the story of the Silver Hoofed Goat comes to an end.

8. The Dwarf in the Storm.

On a dismal night of wind and rain, a poor little dwarf was wandering through the streets of a small town that stood beneath a mountain. The dwarf was seeking shelter; but though he knocked at many doors, no one would open to him. The rain soaked through his ragged cloak and drenched him to the skin, and every now and then a gust of wind would lift him off his feet, and send him spinning to knock his little head against a house door.

'Shelter! Shelter!' he moaned. 'Will no kind person give me shelter?'

But he heard nothing except curses from behind locked doors, and shouts telling him to get him gone.

Just beyond the town, all by itself, stood a little cottage. By the time the dwarf reached it, he was nigh fainting. 'This is my last hope,' he said to himself. 'If they will not take pity on me here, heaven help them.'

And he knocked on the door.

The door was at once opened, and an old man looked out.

'Shelter!' gasped the dwarf.

'Aye, poor soul, come in and welcome!' said the old man. And he drew the dwarf in, and sat him down before a wood fire. Then came the old man's wife, and drew off the dwarf's sodden cloak and wrapped him in a blanket, and set bread and milk and cheese before him, and bade him eat.

The dwarf shook and shivered for a while, and then the life came back to him, and he held out his little bony hands to the blaze.

'Eat,' said the old wife.

The dwarf took a sip of the milk, and a few crumbs of the bread. 'I am not used to this food,' he said, 'and I cannot eat it, but I thank you humbly. And now I must go.'

'*Go!*' said the old man. 'Go out into the storm again! Nay, nay! We are poor folk, and we have but the one bed, and that a hard one. But you are welcome to it, sir; and my old woman and I can sleep sweetly enough before the fire.'

'Again I thank you humbly,' said the dwarf. 'But this night I have business on the mountain top, and I have many miles to go before I reach there. I will think of you tomorrow, and you will think of me.'

And he wrapped himself in his ragged cloak again, and went out into the darkness.

The old couple went to their hard bed and fell asleep.

Early in the morning they were wakened by a brilliant flash of lightning, and then came a tremendous clap of thunder. Rain was rattling on the roof; the wind was howling round the cottage; the whole world seemed to be filled with the roaring and gurgling of water, the boom of the wind, the claps and clattering echoes of thunder, and the flash after flash of lightning.

The old man stumbled to the window and peered out.

'Heaven help us!' he shouted. 'The water is pouring down in rivers from the mountain!'

It was indeed! The mountain seemed to be churned up into a hundred foaming waterfalls that grew bigger and bigger every moment, until the hundred waterfalls met and joined into one great sluice of rushing river, that raged round rocks, and uprooted trees, and poured down and flooded the streets of the town.

'Crash!' Up there on the mountain an enormous rock was dragged from its bed and came roaring and bumping down the mountain, dragging with it tons of earth and stones and a forest of torn-up trees. Carrying all these things in its flood, the river poured over the town:

roofs fell in, walls tumbled, the raging waters closed over the town till not a trace of it was left. And still the river came on, and the huge rock was tossing and whirling in the midst of it.

'May all that is kind preserve us!' cried the old man. 'Say your prayers, old woman; our turn is coming!'

And as they peered fearfully out, what should they see but their little friend the dwarf, dancing up and down on the top of the great rock, and steering it with the trunk of a fir tree as if it had been a ship. On and on came the mighty river, and on and on came the huge rock, and on and on came the dancing dwarf, steering the rock with his tree trunk. He steered the rock till it drew close up against the little house, and there the rock stopped. And the river dashed against the bulk of the rock and divided into two foaming streams; one stream surged to the right of the little house, and the other stream surged to the left of it; but the little house itself stood firm and dry with the great rock to buttress it.

The old couple watched from their window in amazement. The dwarf had flung away the tree trunk and was standing motionless as a statue on the rock. And as they looked at him, they saw that he was growing taller. He grew to the size of a man, he grew to the size of a giant, he grew till his head seemed to touch the clouds. And then he was a cloud himself, with his tattered cloak whirling in wreaths of mist about him. And then the clouds and the mist were gone, and the sun shone from a blue sky, and glittered on the lake of water that covered the town and on the great rock that towered behind the cottage and protected it.

9. *The Old Man and his Three Daughters*

An old man had a little farm, a good wife, and three very beautiful grown up daughters, whose names were Lubaska, Mashka, and Melitsa.

Well now, one morning in early spring the old man went to plough a field. It wasn't at all a pleasant day: the wind was cold, and great dark clouds were hurrying across the sky.

'Eh dear,' said the old man, 'this is enough to chill the marrow in one's bones! If only the sun would show himself, and warm me up a bit! But there, I'm an honest chap, I don't ask favours for nothing. So just you peep out, my lord Sun, and I will give you my Lubaska, my lovely eldest daughter, to be your wife.'

The Sun heard, the Sun laughed. He came out from behind the clouds and warmed the old man through and through.

By and by the old man's eldest daughter, the beautiful Lubaska, came into the field, bringing her father's dinner in a little basket.

'Ah,' said the old man, 'you have come at the right moment, my Lubaska, I have just given you to this kind gentleman, the sun, to be his wife.'

'Oh thank you, little father,' said Lubaska. 'I am indeed honoured!'

Then the Sun took Lubaska in his arms, and lifted her up into the sky. But before he went, he said to the old man, 'We respectfully beg that you will honour us with a visit, when you can spare the time.'

'Yes, yes,' said the old man, 'I will pay you a visit.'

And when he had finished his ploughing he went home.

'But where is Lubaska?' asked the old man's wife.

'I have given her in marriage,' said the old man.

'To whom have you given her?' asked his wife.

'To my lord the Sun,' said the old man.

'Now heaven be thanked!' said the old man's wife. 'That is a truly splendid marriage!'

Some time after this, the old man went to the forest to cut wood. He went and he went, thinking to find better wood farther on. And then he got tired, and sat down under a tree, and fell asleep. When he woke up it was dark night, and he didn't know where he was, or how to find his way home.

'Eh dear,' he said. 'It would be properly kind of the Moon if he would just shine out and show me the way! But being an honest man, I don't ask favours for nothing! So if you, Sir Moon, will but light my way home, I will give you my second daughter, my darling Mashka, to be your wife.'

When the Moon heard that, he laughed till his full round face was all bright with smiles. And he bowed himself down among the forest trees, and guided the old man home.

On his way the old man met his second daughter, Mashka, who had been sent out by her mother to look for him.

'Ah, well met, Mashka my darling!' said the old man. 'See, here is your husband to be – his majesty the Moon. He is a splendid chap, I can tell you! Go, live with him in peace, and don't forget us.'

'No, no, I won't forget you, little father,' said Mashka.

Then the Moon took Mashka up in his gentle arms, and carried her away to his palace on the top of a high mountain.

And the old man went home, well pleased with himself.

'But didn't you meet Mashka?' said his wife. 'I sent her out to look for you.'

'Oh yes, I met her,' said the old man, 'and in a good hour too. I was just having a chat with his majesty the Moon, and I have given Mashka to him in marriage.'

'That is another splendid marriage,' said his wife. 'You have done well, old man.'

The old man chuckled. 'I'm a fellow who knows which side his bread is buttered!' he said. 'But it won't do to neglect my work: tomorrow I must rise early, for the hay in the east meadow is ripe for cutting.'

So next morning the old man rose at dawn, took his scythe, and went to the east meadow to mow the hay. It was very hot, there wasn't a cloud in the sky, and soon the old man was damp with sweat.

'Oh dear,' he said, letting the scythe drop from his hand, 'if only the Wind would be pleased to blow a little, what wouldn't I give him? I would give him my youngest daughter, my darling little Melitsa, to be his wife.'

High over head, the Wind was resting languidly in the blue of the sky. And when he heard what the old man said, he laughed for joy: he stretched himself, he floated down from the sky, he puffed out his cheeks and blew, so gently, so coolly, in the old man's face that it was a pleasure for both of them.

And just as the old man and the wind were hobnobbing together, Melitsa, the old man's youngest daughter – the only one who now remained at home – came into the field, bringing her father's breakfast in a basket.

'Darling little Melitsa,' said the old man, 'you have come at the right moment. This noble fellow, the Wind, and I have become fast friends; and it is you, my darling, who is to be the noble fellow's wife.'

Then the Wind laughed for joy. He kissed Melitsa's rosy lips; he took Melitsa – oh so tenderly – up in his arms, and flew away with her.

When the old man went home that evening, his wife said, 'Did Melitsa stay to help you with the hay that she didn't come home?'

'No, she didn't stay to help me,' chuckled the old man. 'She won't be helping either me or you any more, old woman. I've given her in marriage to the Wind.'

'Well there,' said his wife, 'I suppose you've done right. Girls must be married, and certainly our three have made splendid marriages. But oh dear, deary me, I shall miss them sorely!'

'We can pay them visits from time to time,' said the old man.

But his wife said, 'The Sun lives up in the sky, and the Moon lives on the top of the highest mountain in the world, and the Wind goes whirling all over the earth – how are two old things the likes of you and me to go visiting the likes of them?'

'I don't doubt they'll find a way,' said the old man.

And sure enough, about a week later, a little white cloud came drifting in through the kitchen window; and on the cloud, in glittering golden letters, was written:

'*Darling Mother and darling Father,*

I am so happy with my husband the Sun, and I would like you to pay us a visit. We will send a sunbeam down to fetch you next Monday morning.
Your loving daughter,
Lubaska.'

'There,' said the old man, 'what did I tell you?'

But the old woman said, 'What, me at my age, to go traipsing about on a sunbeam! I should die of fright!'

'Then I'll have to go alone,' said the old man. 'For go I will.'

So on Monday morning, the old man trimmed his beard, washed himself all over at the pump in the back yard, dressed himself in his Sunday coat and trousers, and went to stand outside the garden gate, looking up at the sun. He hadn't long to wait before a sunbeam came flickering down, wrapped itself round him, and carried him up to the Sun's golden palace in the sky.

The Sun received the old man very kindly; and as to Lubaska, it seemed she would never have done hugging and kissing him.

'And now that your father has come,' said the Sun, 'we must give him something nice to eat – what shall it be?'

'Little Father is very fond of pancakes,' said Lubaska.

'Then pancakes let it be,' said the Sun.

So Lubaska got busy mixing the batter. The old man felt puzzled. He looked about – he couldn't see any stove, let alone a fire. Then how was Lubaska going to cook the pancakes? But Lubaska laughed. When the batter was ready, she poured it on the Sun's head – and hey presto! In less than a minute the pancakes were cooked.

'Well!' said the old man, '*Well!* That's something to tell my old woman when I get home!'

He spent a happy day up there in the Sun's palace. They gave him a good dinner, and a good tea; and everything that needed cooking was cooked in the same happy way – on the Sun's fiery head. In the evening a rosy sunbeam carried the old man home again. And as soon as the old man got home, he said to his wife, 'Old woman, make pancakes.'

'Why old man, what are you talking about?' said the old woman. 'Pancakes at this time of night! Can't you see that the fire is out?'

'No matter for that,' said the old man. 'Just you mix the batter.'

So the old woman mixed the batter. And then the old man said, 'Now pour it on my head.'

'Are you gone clean crazy?' said the old woman.

'Do as you're told,' said the old man quite fiercely.

So the old woman poured the batter on to the old man's head.

My word, what a mess! The batter plastered up the old man's eyes and his nose and his ears – he spent half the night washing himself clean again – and he sulked all the next day.

Well, it wasn't long after this when the old man decided to visit Mashka, his second daughter – she who had married the Moon. His old wife didn't want him to go, but go he would. He set out early one morning; he walked all day, and in the evening came to the Moon's palace at the top of a high mountain. It was a fine evening, and the Moon and Mashka were lying asleep on a bed of white lilies outside the palace. They looked so happy and comfortable that the old man scarcely liked to waken them; but after all he had come a very long way, and he was tired and thirsty. So, after saying 'ahem! ahem!' several times without any result, he bent down and gave Mashka's arm a pinch.

Mashka woke; at first she was annoyed; but when she saw who had pinched her, she laughed delightedly, clapped her hands, and woke the Moon.

'See, see, husband,' she said. 'Here is my dear old daddy come to pay us a visit!'

The Moon woke, shedding his soft silvery light far and wide. He led the old man into his palace, where there was no need of lamps or candles, for his bland smiling face lit up every corridor and room they passed through. In his small cosy study, where pictures of all the stars of heaven decorated the walls, he bade the old man be seated and said to his wife, 'Mashka, my darling, our little father must be hungry and thirsty after his long journey. Go into the cellar and bring up a bottle of our best wine, and also a jar of honey and a loaf of your own baking.'

Mashka went down into the cellar. She had no need of a lamp, for the Moon stood at the top of the cellar steps holding out his finger, and the finger lit up the way more brightly than the brightest candle.

So, gobbling bread and honey, and drinking down such heady and delicious wine as is not to be found anywhere else on earth, the old man spent a happy night with the Moon and Mashka, and fell asleep towards morning – and woke to find himself back in his own little farm house, for the kind Moon had taken him up in his gentle arms, and carried him home.

'Wife,' said the old man, 'I fancy bread and honey for my breakfast.'

'But we haven't any honey,' said his wife.

'Nonsense!' said the old man. 'There's sure to be a jarful in the cellar. Just you go down and fetch it up.'

The old woman was going to light a candle, but the old man said, 'No, no, none of that! *I'll* give you a light!'

And he went to the top of the cellar steps, and held out his fore-finger.

Well, of course the finger gave no light at all, and so the old woman told him. But the stubborn old fellow said that it must and did give a light. And the result of it all was that the old woman, fumbling her way down in the dark, fell head over heels, and sprained her ankle, and was laid up for some time.

The old man couldn't understand it: no, he simply couldn't. But he nursed his old wife very devotedly. And when she was able to walk about again, he suggested that they should both set out to pay a visit to their third daughter, Melitsa, she who had married the Wind.

But the old woman said, 'After your visit to the Sun *you* got a messed up head; after your visit to the Moon *I* got a sprained ankle. Seems to me that we'd best stay at home.'

'Third time's lucky,' said the old man. 'And if you won't come with me, I shall go alone.'

So he set out. He hadn't so far to go this time. The Wind lived in a fine big manor house on the bank of a river; and the old man, having risen early, reached this house soon after midday. His welcome from the Wind was friendly as could be, and from his daughter Melitsa it was rapturous. The first thing they did was to give the old man a good meal; and when the old man had eaten and rested a while, the Wind said, 'Fetch your mantle, Melitsa, and we will take Little Father for a sail on the river.'

So Melitsa fetched her mantle, which was woven of bird's feathers, and the Wind laid the mantle on the water, lifted the old man and Melitsa on to it, and sat down on it himself. Then he blew with his breath, gently, gently, and the mantle sailed down the river, and up the river again, and across to the other side of the river and back, going just whichever way the Wind's breath guided it.

'This is truly the one and only way to go sailing!' exclaimed the old man. 'A fig for sails, a fig for oars, a fig for clumsy great boats! You, my dear son-in-law, have taught me a thing or two!'

But all good things must come to an end. And at sunset the Wind blew the mantle on to the shore again. Then he took the old man up in his arms and carried him home.

Now you must know that not far from the old man's farm was a lake. And next morning, directly after breakfast, the old man said, 'Wife, go upstairs and bring down your best cloak, the one you wear on Sundays, so that we may go for a sail on the lake.'

'*A sail on the lake!*' exclaimed the old woman. 'Have you got a hole in the back of your silly old head? And has the last little bit of sense you possess dropped through the hole and fallen heaven knows where? How can we go for a sail on the lake when we haven't a boat?'

'You just fetch your cloak and leave the rest to me,' said the old man. 'Am I master in my own house, or am I not?'

Well, the old woman grumbled like anything, but she fetched the cloak. And the old man tucked it under his arm, took his wife by the hand, and went with her to the lake. Then he threw the cloak on to the water, and said, 'Jump!'

'*No!*' said the old woman.

'Jump, I say!' cried the old man.

He gave her such a push that willy-nilly she had to jump. And he jumped after her on to the cloak.

What happened? Well of course the cloak sank under their weight, and down they went, down under the water – cloak, old woman, and old man – down to the bottom of the lake.

Were they drowned? No, they weren't. For by good chance the Wind was coming that way, and he saw what had happened. So he blew a mighty breath which parted the water to the right and left in huge waves, and then he caught up the old man and the old woman and carried them home.

The old woman had had a rare fright. She thanked the Wind again and again for coming to their rescue. But when the Wind had gone, she turned furiously on the old man.

'Now you see what comes of trying to ape your betters!' she said. 'First you nigh choke yourself with batter, then you nearly break my ankle, and then you do your best to drown us both! Will you never learn sense?'

'Well, I'll own things didn't turn out in just the way they should,' said the old man. 'But if we didn't experiment a bit, we should never get any farther, we should just remain plain numbskulls for the rest of our lives.'

'Better be numbskulls and live in peace!' said the old woman.

'I shall never agree with that,' said the old man.

So they argued for many a day. But which of them had the rights of it, is more than I can tell you.

10. The Gypsy and the Dragon

A gypsy was wandering through the world. He was a handsome young fellow, with his curly brown hair and his big dark eyes, and his strong, well-shaped limbs. He had been walking all day, and now it was evening. So, as he was going through a wood, he sat down to rest under a sweet chestnut tree.

Up on a branch, high above the gypsy's head, a little bird was singing its goodnight song. '*Chip-a-wee, chip-a-wee, chee-chee-chee-chee!*'

The gypsy looked up – oh such a pretty little bird! And now the little bird was hopping down from branch to branch. Now it was perched on the very lowest branch of the tree; and it was cocking its head on one side, and looking at the gypsy out of one bright eye.

'Yes,' said the little bird, after it had looked the gypsy over very carefully. 'Yes, I think you'll do.'

And it flew right down, and perched on the gypsy's knee. 'Be so good as to pull a feather out of my right wing,' said the little bird.

'Oh,' said the gypsy, 'why should I do that?'

'Because I say so,' said the little bird, in a very commanding sort of voice. 'Now, now, do as you're told.'

'But it might hurt you, my little bird.'

'What of that?' said the little bird. 'A moment's hurt for a lifetime of good and happiness!'

'Well, I suppose you know what you're talking about,' said the gypsy, 'But I certainly don't.'

'You will, you will,' said the little bird. 'Come, don't be a fool!'

'I am *not* a fool, I never *was* a fool,' said the gypsy indignantly. And feeling annoyed, he pulled a feather out of the little bird's right wing.

'Good lad, good lad!' cried the little bird. 'Mind you keep that feather carefully. It's very precious. You have but to touch it with your finger, and it will give you the power of knowing what people are thinking about you. And that's a gift that few possess. Now go to sleep. In the morning you must journey on until you come to the king's capital city. There's a task waiting for you, my lad; and the feather will help you to carry out that task. Goodnight! Sleep well!'

Then the little bird flew away. And the gypsy, having put the feather in his pocket, lay down to sleep.

He woke in the morning feeling strong and vigorous. Hard beds and chilly nights were nothing to him – he was used to them. He had some bread and cheese and a bottle of beer in his knapsack. So he ate and drank. And then, springing to his feet, he set off merrily for the king's capital city. 'May as well go there as anywhere else,' he said to himself. 'And a bird that can talk is a thing one doesn't meet with every day. So, my little bird, yours to command!'

An hour's walking brought him to the city. And there he got a surprise. For a sadder place than that city surely couldn't exist on earth! The shops were all shut, the house doors were all closed, the streets were more or less empty; and the few people that the gypsy met were shedding tears.

'What's the matter here? Why do you weep?' asked the gypsy, stopping this person and that. But they only shook their heads and passed on without answering him.

So, as he reached the end of one street, and was just turning into another street, he came face to face with a dignified old gentleman. The old gentleman was dabbing at his eyes with a handkerchief, wiping away the tears that filled them. 'Oh,' thought the old gentleman, looking at the gypsy, 'here's a hard-hearted fellow! He doesn't shed a single tear!'

And the gypsy, thanks to the little bird's feather, which he now remembered to touch with his right forefinger, knew what the old gentleman was thinking.

'No man has ever accused me of being hard-hearted before,' said the gypsy indignantly. 'But on this bright morning I see no cause for shedding tears.'

'No cause!' exclaimed the old gentleman. *'No cause!* And this very morning our beautiful princess, the king's only child, the heir to the throne, has been carried off by a dragon! Nine years ago this mighty dragon threatened to destroy the city, unless the king signed a contract promising to give him every year an eighteen-year-old maiden. The king signed the contract – well, what else could he do? The maidens were chosen each year by lot. And this year – oh, alack the day! – the lot fell upon our beautiful princess, the heir to the throne, the king's only daughter. The king would have sent another maiden in her stead, but – ah, the noble girl – she said, "It is I who am chosen, it is I who must go." Nothing would dissuade her. And when the dragon came rushing, she was there, in the appointed place outside the city gates, waiting for him. And he seized her up and carried her off, and so – '

'And isn't there one among you valiant enough to fight and kill the dragon?' cried the gypsy.

'There have been many valiant enough,' answered the old lord. 'But there have been none strong enough. Alack, poor souls, they have fought and died, fought and died.'

'Then I will both fight and conquer that dragon!' cried the gypsy. 'Bring me to the king that I may speak with him.'

So the old lord led the gypsy to the king, whom they found in his palace, sitting alone in a small room, and weeping as all his subjects were weeping.

'May it please your majesty,' said the old lord, 'I have brought you yet one more valiant lad who seeks to fight and kill the dragon.'

The king leaped to his feet. His eyes were shining with a desperate hope. 'I will give you armour,' he cried. 'I will give you weapons – sword, spear. bow, arrows, money, a horse. . .'

'Nay,' said the gypsy, 'what should I do weighed down with all that gear? Give me a sword and a good horse to ride, that is all I ask. . . . Oh and maybe a decent jerkin and hose, since it were well to make a good impression on one's enemy. And also, as to fight on an empty stomach puts one at a disadvantage, I should be grateful for a meal before I set out.'

All that he asked for, the gypsy got. And after a good meal, he mounted the horse that the king had ordered for him, and set off, feeling very proud of himself, and looking very handsome in his new jerkin and hose, and with a sharp sword in its sheath at his belt. He had a long ride; it took him eleven days to reach the dragon's castle. But the king had provided him with a purse full of money, and he was able to put up at inns on the way – inns where every host greeted him with pitying looks, as of one doomed to destruction.

But the more sadly the innkeepers shook their heads, the more stubbornly the gypsy's courage rose. He thought of the little bird. Hadn't the little bird said, 'There is a task waiting for you'? Hadn't the little bird given him a feather to help him perform that task?

He had faith in the little bird – surely it would not send him to his death!

So, full of hope and courage, the gypsy rode on his way, and on the eleventh day came to the dragon's castle. The castle stood grimly on top of a low rocky hill, under a range of mountains. The windows of the castle were all shuttered and barred, except one. And the gypsy, looking up, saw the dragon inside that window, coiled on a sofa, and staring out at him.

'What, yet another of you!' roared the dragon, putting his head out of the window. The roaring voice was like a gale of wind, the gale of wind toppled the gypsy off his horse, and flung the horse to the ground. The horse scrambled to his feet and galloped off. The gypsy scrambled to his feet and glared up at the dragon.

'Another time,' said he, 'take care to greet your guests more politely, or it will be the worse for you! I see you are strong, but I see that you are also stupid. Now *I* am the strongest man on earth. And I am also the cleverest.'

'Then show your strength, show your cleverness, show your power!' roared the dragon. 'Roar so loud that *I* shall topple to the ground!'

'Nay,' said the gypsy, 'that I won't! Should *I* roar, your castle would fall to the ground, and you would be squashed to death under it. Now I have no objection to *your* being squashed to death; but I don't wish to destroy your castle, which pleases me. So, on the whole, we will leave things as they are.'

'Oh ho, little mannikin, oh ho!' snorted the dragon. 'Just you wait!
I'll come down, and we'll match trick to trick – then we'll soon see
which of us is cleverest!'

Then the dragon gave a leap through the window; and landed on his
four scaly feet close to the gypsy.

The gypsy's heart was thumping against his ribs. Yes, truly for a
moment he was terrified. But he managed to conceal his terror, and to
put on a brave smile. 'Well, old stupid,' he said, 'What now?'

'Come with me,' said the dragon, 'and *I'll* show you. . .! And I'm no
more stupid than you are,' he added defiantly.

'That remains to be proved,' said the gypsy. 'But lead on.'

Grunting and breathing fire, the dragon led the way up one of the
mountains, and the gypsy followed. Part way up they came to a
plateau, and there the dragon stopped. On the plateau lay a pile of
huge stones.

'How much would you say each of these stones weighs?' said the
dragon.

'Not less than a ton, certainly,' said the gypsy.

'Then just you watch!' said the dragon.

And he seized up one stone after another and flung them into the air.
He flung them so high that they vanished in the clouds; and as they came
hurtling down again, he caught them as easily as if they had been rubber
balls, and again threw them up, and again caught them as they came
down, in such a wild, whirling kind of game as made the gypsy feel quite
giddy.

'*There!*' said the dragon triumphantly. 'Can you match that, Mr
Call-Yourself-Clever?'

The gypsy shrugged his shoulders. 'If the stones were lumps of gold,'
he said, 'it might amuse me to play with them. But with common dirty
lumps of granite I will not soil my hands.'

The dragon grunted. He didn't quite know what to make of the
gypsy. He had never met anyone like him before. 'Don't you feel like
running away?' he said.

'*Run away?*' said the gypsy. 'Why should I do that?'

'Most people do,' said the dragon.

'But I am not "most people,"' answered the gypsy.

'I like to pounce, I like to pounce,' growled the dragon. 'But I can't
pounce if you don't run.'

'I'm waiting for you to show me your next trick,' said the gypsy. 'You

show me your tricks today, and tomorrow I'll show you mine. And won't you get the surprise of your life – oh, won't you!'

The dragon was beginning to feel uneasy. He led the way on round the mountain until they came to a large lake – so large a lake that there was no seeing across it.

'Now watch!' said the dragon.

And lying flat he plunged his snout into the lake. One gulp – he swallowed down all the water. Where the lake had been there was nothing now but an immense number of fishes, flapping about on the wet mud.

The dragon spat the water out again. There was the lake once more, with the fish swimming in it. 'I'll wager you can't match that, young fellow,' he said.

'Pooh!' said the gypsy. 'When I was a small child I drank at one sitting as much as would fill that lake three times over – it was on my fifth birthday, I remember. You'll have to show me some better trick than that!'

'So I will then,' said the dragon.

And he led the gypsy into a meadow that was covered with poppies. He stamped three times on the ground, and from every poppy there sprang up an armed man. Drawing their swords this great throng of men rushed on the dragon. But he gave each of them a slap on the head – and they all sank down into the earth and vanished.

'Well, well,' said the gypsy, 'if you've nothing but this child's play to show me, we may as well go back to your castle. You'd do well to take some rest before we hold our fight. But I warn you, you'll have your work cut out. Last year, when I was up in the moon visiting my cousin, I ate up three thousand dragon kings. And I could have eaten up as many more – only you see there weren't any more. . . But it's getting late. Come on now, back we go! Tonight to eat and sleep, tomorrow to fight. You can give me a bed in your castle, I suppose?'

'Yes, I can give you a bed,' said the dragon, who was beginning to feel frightened. In fact he was trembling. 'This is no end of a fellow,' he thought. 'It were better not to fight him. Tonight, when he sleeps, I will creep into his room and kill him.'

But the gypsy had in his pocket the feather which the little bird had given him: the feather, if you remember, that told him what people were thinking about him. Now he put his hand in his pocket and touched the feather.

'Ha, ha, master dragon,' said he. 'I'll show you a trick that you couldn't do. I'll tell you what you were thinking a moment ago.'

'You can't do that,' growled the dragon.

'Oh can't I?' laughed the gypsy. 'How about this then?. . . "No end of a fellow. . . Tonight when he is asleep I will creep into his room and kill him."'

'I didn't, I never did think anything of the sort!' cried the dragon. But he was thinking to himself, 'The lad is a wizard in disguise – my end is near!'

'And now,' laughed the gypsy, 'you're thinking that your end is near. And never did you have a truer thought. Unless, of course, you will do as I tell you.'

'But – but wh-what must I do?' wailed the dragon.

'Take yourself off to the end of the world,' said the gypsy, 'and never come back. There's a nice lot of room at the end of the world, so I've heard. And you can amuse yourself there by building a new castle. . . I daresay the lobsters will help you build – that is of course if you treat them politely. . . Hullo, hullo! You're off, are you? Well goodbye, and a pleasant journey!'

The dragon spread his great scaly wings and flew away. The gypsy laughed and turned to go into the castle. . . But what did he hear, and what did he see? He heard the *clipper-clop* of horses' hoofs; and out from the gates of the castle courtyard came eight lovely girls, riding on eight snow-white horses. Now they were leaping off their horses, now they were surrounding the gypsy, now they were kneeling at his feet, kissing his hands and the hem of his tunic.

'Hail, hail to our best, our bravest, our dearest deliverer!' they cried.

The gypsy looked from one lovely girl to another. 'Which of you is the princess?' he asked. 'It is the princess who should lead this glad procession home.'

'We don't know where the princess is,' said one of the girls. 'Last night she was here with us in the castle, but this morning she had disappeared. Oh, we've searched for her everywhere. I assure you she is not in the castle.'

'Then I suppose we may as well ride back to the city,' said the gypsy. But he was bitterly disappointed.

He had been feeling so proud of himself. And now – what was he to say to the king? 'The dragon is banished to the end of the world, he will trouble you no more – but your daughter is lost.' Would the king thank him for such news as that? – And the tiresome little bird who had promised him a lifetime of good and happiness! How could there be any good or happiness for him, unless he could restore the princess to her father?

So in a sombre mood he mounted his horse, which had run up to him whinnying directly it saw him, and the little procession set off on the long ride back to the king's city, the eight lovely girls singing happy songs, the gypsy downcast and thoughtful.

At the city gates he parted from the girls, leaving them to go in and rejoin their parents. He himself rode on his way to find the little bird in the wood. He wanted to ask the little bird about the princess.

As he rode he heard first merry peal after merry peal of the church bells, as the citizens welcomed the return of the maidens; and then the sudden stop of those merry peals. . . and then a solemn tolling.

'Yes,' thought the gypsy, 'they have just realized that the princess is missing. They are tolling out their sorrow.'

Full of distress and bitter disappointment, he rode on to the wood, and into the wood, and came to the sweet chestnut tree.

'*Chip-a-wee, chip-a-wee, chee-chee-chee-chee!*' That was the little bird singing up in the tree. But the gypsy had no eyes for the little bird, because under the tree sat the most beautiful maiden. Yes, none other than the princess, the king's lovely daughter.

'The meeting of true lovers should not be seen by any eyes but mine,' said the little bird, flying down from the tree. 'And so I have brought the princess here. Come, my gypsy lad, kiss her, take her up in your arms, lift her on to your horse, and carry her back to her father. All is well now, all is well, nothing remains but to live happily ever after.'

So the princess kissed the gypsy, and the gypsy kissed the princess, and lifted her up in front of him on to his horse, and rode back with her to her father, the king. The little bird flew over their heads to the end of the wood. The last they heard of it was its merry song, 'Happy ever after! Happy ever after! That's the way good stories end. Happy ever after!'

And that's how our story does end. The gypsy married the princess, and in course of time became king. He made a good, merry and wise king, and all his subjects loved him.

You see, he still had the little bird's feather. And to know what people are thinking and feeling about you is a great help when it comes to ruling over them.

11. *The Miller and the Devil*

On a fine summer evening, a miller and a shepherd were sitting on a bench outside an inn, chatting together over their mugs of beer, when they saw a lord and lady drive past in a splendid coach.

'See that!' said the miller. 'How unfair it is! Those fine folk neither toil nor spin, and yet they own the earth. Whereas I have to toil week in week out, from early Monday morning to late on Saturday afternoon, just to keep body and soul together. Oh if I were but rich I shouldn't care where the money came from; no, not even if the Devil himself should give it to me!'

'If that's how you feel,' said the shepherd, 'it's easily managed. All you have to do is to sell your soul to Satan. I'm sure that in return he will be delighted to oblige you with any amount of money – more than you can possibly spend.'

'But how can I sell my soul to him?' asked the miller. 'I've never seen him, and I don't know where to find him.'

The shepherd shrugged his shoulders and laughed. He was a merry fellow. 'I'm fairly often in Satan's company,' he said. 'Just you write a note to him, and I'll see that he gets it.'

So the miller got pen and paper from the inn's landlord, and wrote at the shepherd's dictation:

'*I, Makin the miller, promise to render up my soul to Satan at the end of seven years, if during those seven years Satan will provide me with as much money as I can possibly spend.*'

And the shepherd took the note and delivered it that night to Satan.

Next morning, when the miller got up, what did he see? On the floor of every room in his house were great sacks, standing so close together that there was scarcely space to walk between them. And every sack was full to the brim with gold coins. And when he went down to his mill, there too he found sacks full of gold stacked up everywhere.

The miller laughed, the miller shed tears, he felt half crazy with joy. From that day onward he did no more work. But he didn't give up his mill, lest people should talk. He employed men to work for him, whilst he himself drove about in a carriage finer than my lord's, and wore a new suit of clothes every day.

So he lived without a care for seven years. And then one morning, when he was down at the mill, lording it over his work people, he looked out of a little round window, and saw two tall men coming along the lane that led to the mill. One of the men was carrying a black sack, the other was holding up a piece of paper, which he was twirling round and round his forefinger. The miller hastily shut the window, for there was something about those two men that set his heart fluttering in wild panic. But the two men, lightly leaping, came right in through the window pane, and to his horror the miller saw that each man had a long tail neatly coiled through a hole in the seat of his trousers. And the man who was carrying the sack gave a grin and said, 'Time's up, master miller.'

'No!' cried the miller. '*No, no, no!*'

But the man who was twirling the paper said, 'Your letter and your signature, I believe, sir – a seven years' contract which ends today.'

And the two of them caught hold of the miller, bundled him into the sack, and carried him off between them, through the window, and along the lane, and away and away on the road to Hell.

And as they went they passed a field where the shepherd was tending his sheep. The shepherd heard the miller shouting inside the sack.

'Dear me,' said the shepherd to himself, 'I'm afraid this is my doing! Poor fellow – no, Satan shan't have him!'

But what could the shepherd do? He looked up the road and saw two peasants coming along, carrying their garden produce to market. And since the shepherd knew some magic he so arranged it that these two peasants began to quarrel. I can't tell you what the quarrel was about, but it grew more and more violent. Now the peasants were shouting and

hitting out at each other. And when the devils saw this, they set down the sack they were carrying, and ran joyfully to join in the quarrel.

So there were the four of them, the two devils and the two peasants, yelling and cursing and fisticuffing: and there was the sack dumped down under the hedge. The shepherd didn't waste a moment, he ran to the sack, cut the cord that bound the neck of it, let out the miller, called to his big dog, put the dog in the sack, and tied the sack up again. 'Be off and hide behind the hedge,' he said to the miller. 'And as you value your soul, *keep still.*'

Then he went back to his sheep again.

So, when the two devils and the two peasants had wearied of their squabbling, the two peasants went on their way, and the two devils picked up the sack, and strolled off to Hell, where Satan was waiting to receive his latest capture, the miller.

'Ha! ha! ha!' We have the miller!' laughed Satan. And 'Ha! ha! ha!' laughed a crowd of devils, dancing round the sack. 'Seven years of riches, seven years of riches, and seven million times seven million years to seethe in Satan's cauldron!'

'Stand back!' shouted Satan. 'I myself will have the pleasure of releasing our prisoner the miller!'

And he stooped and untied the cord round the end of the sack. '*Gr-re! Re-re!*' Out leaped the shepherd's great dog. '*Gr-gr-grrr!*' The dog seized Satan's tail and bit off the end of it; he leaped upon one devil, he leaped upon another devil, snarling and biting. The devils screamed, the devils ran. Satan was hollering for some ointment to put on his bleeding tail, all Hell was pandemonium. And the great dog rushed out of Hell gate and returned to the shepherd.

But that very hour Satan made a new law: from henceforth, and forever, no miller was to be allowed to enter Hell.

12. The Fiddler in Hell

One night a Fiddler, who had been at a merrymaking in the town, was strolling home. But the night was dark, and the Fiddler was heedless. He came to a hole in the road, and fell through it. Where did he fall to? Down, down, down into Hell.

The Fiddler blinked and looked about him. Hullo, hullo, here was someone he knew! It was old Peribondi who had been in his life a very rich man, and had entertained at his table the grandest people in the neighbourhood. Old Peribondi had often engaged the Fiddler to play for him during those dinners, and after the dinners, when the grandees amused themselves by dancing in Peribondi's great hall.

And here was poor old Peribondi sitting in a tub of fire, with only his head and neck sticking out!

'Oh sir, oh sir,' said the Fiddler, 'it grieves me to the soul to see you here! I cannot understand how it has come about – and you in your life so generous and open-handed!'

'No, no,' groaned old Peribondi, 'not generous. Only flattered to entertain and be made much of by the rich. To the poor folk of earth I never gave a halfpenny, and if such folk came begging to my door, I had them driven away with whips. And so I am justly punished. I am beaten with rods, I am torn by the demons' long nails; and as if that were not enough, I am made to sit for hours on end in this tub of fire.

'But, Fiddler, I hoarded as well as spent. I filled two large barrels to the brim with money. One I filled with gold coins, the other I filled with silver coins. These barrels I hid; the one filled with gold coins I buried under the gateway of my house; the one filled with silver coins I buried under the floor of my stables. Fiddler, if ever you get out of this accursed place, go to my three sons, tell them where the money is buried, bid them dig up the barrels, and distribute the money among the poor and needy. Ah, if this is done, perhaps the Lord of Heaven will forgive me, and lift me out of my misery, and permit me to creep into some humble corner of Paradise . . . Oh see, here they come, the devils, the devils, with their whips of flame to beat and torment me!'

And, with screams of laughter and mocking howls, in rushed hundreds of devils through the open gates of Hell.

'Ah, our little pet, Peribondi!' shrieked the devils. 'See him there, so prettily sitting in his fiery tub! Come, let us pinch him with our burning fingers! Let us scratch him with our long nails, that his howls may make music for our listening ears! But – see there, who is this – a new soul for us to torment?'

'Certainly not!' said the Fiddler indignantly. 'I am an honest fiddler, who has so far lived a blameless life. You must blame the moon, not me, for my coming here. If the moon had been shining as she ought, I should never –'

'A fiddler!' screamed the devils. 'Ah ha, what luck! Play up now, Fiddler, give us some pretty music that we may dance!'

So the Fiddler, very willing to divert the devils' attention from the poor old suffering Peribondi, sat down on an upturned tub, and began to play. And the devils joined hands in a ring round him, and began to dance. My word, how they danced! Leaping high, kicking out their legs, waving their fiery arms, snapping their long-nailed fingers, screaming with laughter, and showing all their gleaming, sharp-pointed teeth. They forgot all about Peribondi, they didn't bother to stoke up the fire in his tub. And the flames in the tub died down and went out, so poor old Peribondi was for the time being eased of his torment.

For three years the Fiddler played without ceasing, and the devils danced without ceasing. And then the Fiddler laid aside his fiddle and asked for a cup of wine, for his mouth was very dry. And they brought him a cup of wine, and he drank it, and prepared to play again.

'There is some mystery about this, little brothers,' he said to the devils. 'Up on earth I could scarcely play for one evening without breaking a string; but down here I play on and on, and the strings remain whole, thanks be to God!'

And as soon as he said those words, 'Thanks be to God,' *snap* – all the strings of his fiddle broke.

What a calamity! 'It seems I shall have to leave you for a while, my friends,' said the Fiddler. 'I must go back up to earth, and get my fiddle fitted out with new strings.'

'No need for that!' cried one of the devils. And he rushed away and

came back with a handful of catgut, which he busied himself fitting on to the fiddle.

But when the Fiddler took up his bow to play again – what happened? *Twang*! Every string broke.

Again and again the devils tried to fit the fiddle with new strings, and again and again the strings broke. The devils stamped and howled in their disappointment, like a nursery full of naughty children – they did so want to go on dancing! They agreed at last to let the Fiddler go up to earth and get new strings for his fiddle; but they sent a devil with him to keep an eye on him, and to make sure of his coming back. And whether it was a long way, or a short way they had to go, the Fiddler and his guardian devil were up on earth again, and had arrived in the Fiddler's native village, before you could count ten.

Now it so happened that on that day a friend of the Fiddler's was getting married. And when the new strings had been fitted on to the fiddle, the Fiddler said to his attendant devil, 'After the wedding there will be a feast. Let us go to the wedding; then we shall be invited to the feast. And after the feast I will strike up a merry tune on my fiddle, and all the people will dance. There will be plenty of pretty girls, and if you disguise yourself as a handsome lad, you can take your pick of those pretty girls for partners – what do you say, old fellow, doesn't that appeal to you?'

It did appeal to the devil; he snapped his fingers, and there in a moment he stood, as pretty a young lad as you could wish to see, and dressed in the smartest of smart tunic and hose.

'Now let us go,' said the devil, smirking at himself in a little glass that he carried in his pocket. 'But we must remember to be back before cockcrow.'

'Ha! Cockcrow is a long way off!' laughed the Fiddler.

And he led the devil among his friends, who were just then coming out of church.

'Fiddler, Fiddler, where have you been all this long while?' cried his friends.

'Oh in many strange places,' said the Fiddler. 'But you see I haven't forgotten you. Allow me to introduce my friend to you – Mr Unbeknown, whom I met on my travels. He won't lack partners when the time comes for dancing. He's as neat on his toes as the devil himself!'

'Ha! ha! ha!' laughed the Fiddler's friends.

So the Fiddler and the disguised devil took their seats at the wedding feast. And after the feast was ended, and the table cleared and pushed back against the wall, the Fiddler sat in a corner and began to play. And they all began to dance.

Some of them danced well, some of them danced not so well; but of all the dancers, none could compare in elegance or grace with the Fiddler's friend, 'Mr Unbeknown.' Every girl in the room was eager to have him for a partner, and the bride herself paid him such attention as *nearly* brought on a fit of sulks in her newly-married husband.

So they made merry throughout the evening, taking no thought of time. Clocks ticked on, struck midnight, struck one o'clock, struck two o'clock, three o'clock, four – and still the company danced, and still the Fiddler played for them, until the eastern sky grew bright, the cocks began to crow, and 'Mr Unbeknown', having gallantly handed his latest partner to a seat, strolled over to the Fiddler and whispered:

> '*Dawn in the sky,*
> *Back to Hell we must fly.*'

The Fiddler smiled. 'Pity to break up the party,' he said.

And he went on playing, and the company went on dancing.

'*Cock-a-doodle doo! Cock-a-doodle-doo-oo-oo!*' The cocks crowing louder, more insistently.

One dance ended, another about to begin: the pretty girls making eyes at the fascinating stranger, Mr Unbeknown, each one anxious to be chosen as his next partner. But now Mr Unbeknown wasn't heeding the pretty girls, nor was he dancing. He was standing at the Fiddler's side, scowling and whispering in his ear, 'Come, come! Enough of this nonsense!'

'Just one more tune,' said the Fiddler. 'Our friends are enjoying themselves so much.'

And he went on playing. And the company went on dancing.

Mr Unbeknown's brows were frowning, Mr Unbeknown's lips were twitching. Mr Unbeknown was pulling at the Fiddler's sleeve. Mr Unbeknown was muttering in the Fiddler's ear. 'Come, you rogue, come!'

But the Fiddler shook Mr Unbeknown's hand off his sleeve, and went on playing, until, with a loud howl, Mr Unbeknown gave a leap through the window and hurried back to Hell.

The Fiddler laid down his bow and laughed. 'My friends,' said he, 'there is an old saying about entertaining angels unawares: but it may surprise you to know that *you*, unawares, have been entertaining a devil.'

And whilst they all crowded round him, he told them his story. 'Now,' said he, when his story was ended, 'just one more dance, and so to bed!'

But that last dance was not a very hearty affair, for though the Fiddler was now in high spirits, the rest of the company were more than a little shaken by what he had told them.

So at last the Fiddler stopped playing, and they all went home. All, that is, except the Fiddler, who went to call on old Peribondi's three sons, to tell them about meeting poor old Peribondi in Hell, and to give them their father's message.

The three sons were good lads; they did exactly what their father had desired: they dug up the barrels, and distributed the money among the poor. But they each kept just one gold coin for themselves, not to spend, but to remind them of their father, and to hold between their clasped hands as they knelt down and prayed to Heaven for his deliverance from that tub of fire.

As for the Fiddler, he left the three brothers to their prayers, and went to the priest, to tell him also the sad story of Peribondi.

And the priest knelt down and prayed for the soul of Peribondi, and the Fiddler knelt down and prayed with him. And all these prayers were heard in Heaven. And the Lord of Heaven sent an angel down into Hell.

At the sight of the angel, the devils ran to hide themselves in corners. And the angel lifted poor old Peribondi out of the tub of fire, and carried him up to heaven, where in some quiet nook he lived in peace ever after.